The Realms Series

Book Two

NEVERLAND

Emory R. Frie

Hannah—
Never grow up, my friend!
With love,
Emory R. Frie

Neverland by Emory R. Frie
www.emoryrfrie.weebly.com
Cover Design: Emory R. Frie
Cover Images © Shutterstock
Paperback ISBN: 978-0-9974354-2-9

For MOM, who taught me to fly.
Without her, I never would've found my NEVERLAND.

Just a boy, Just a child,
In a place where no one grows up;

Young bodies with old minds,
Dream and nightmare reign side by side,
In a place where no one grows up;

A time when darkness shrouded the sun,
Vengeance birthed from sea and blood,
Many had fallen in the war never won,
In a place where no one grows up;

When the boy's heart grieved he became more of a man,
When the pirate's heart hardened with the loss of his hand,
One dreadful night everything changed and feuds began,
Now the ghosts from their mistakes are tied to this land,
In a place where no one grows up;

Just a boy, just a child, in appearance it's true,
But children can carry terrible burdens too,
For sometimes stopping time doesn't mean forever youth,
Living, forgetting, loving, seething, bearing an all too heavy
truth;

Just a boy, Just a child,
In a place where no one grows up.

-Wendy Darling

CHAPTER ONE
LOST GIRL

She looked up to see the Island looming before her.

It's about time, she thought.

The boat rocked back and forth on the waves. The wind rustled through her black hair. It had been a long time since she'd last been to Neverland. For most of her life, she lived on the sea. She never got sea sick, though most would have been green from the way her small boat was tossed among the waves. Nor was she afraid of the sea and its watery depths. With everything that lurked beneath the surface, not one sea monster frightened her.

She'd spent her whole life training for this moment when she would return to Neverland. It had to be convincing. It had to be perfect. And now was the time to set their plans into action.

It had taken months of eating little to nothing so as to get her cheeks to hollow and her ribs to stick out as she looked then. She didn't brush her hair for just as long so as to get it tangled and matted. The clothes on her back were purposefully worn and torn. All in all, her appearance would be believable.

The rickety old boat she sat in had been stolen. It was one of the Lost Boats that washed on the shores of Neverland to deliver Lost Boys. Only those who were hopelessly lost and unloved were sent for and accepted by Neverland. The Lost Boats only brought boys, however. It would've been much easier if she was a boy. But since she wasn't, she needed to be the first official Lost Girl. At least, she needed Pan to think that.

• • •

The girl looked with sharp brown eyes at the quickly approaching island. The waters became more vigorous as the Island pulled her closer. She got the vague suspicion that the mermaids were behind the roughness. But she knew that was impossible. They could never leave the lagoon.

But perhaps the reason the waters were so rough was because the Island was hesitant to accept her. It probably suspected an imposter. But she knew Neverland would let her in. She had been there before. It would let her pass.

The boat washed ashore, lodging itself in the sand. She smirked slightly. She was right. The Island couldn't refuse her.

It can't refuse one of its own.

She stayed in the boat, looking over the sandy beach. Old remnants of Lost Boats were scattered about the shore. Most of the water beaten wood had been there for a long time, even longer than she'd been alive. She was, after all, much older than she looked. A few boats were still intact, though most were but skeletons that had laid there for decades or even centuries. It was hard to tell with Neverland.

A boy stood on the shores, the jungle stretching out behind him. Though he was more of a young man now, she knew never to call him a man no matter his appearance. His auburn hair was naturally a wild mess, his eyes a light brown; not anywhere near the same shade as hers. The clothes on his back were dark green and brown to help him blend in with Neverland's foliage.

She pretended to be frightened, though she supposed it wasn't entirely an act. At least for now she needed to be timid and frail.

The boy seemed confused as he walked over to the boat, and she supposed it was rightly so. Never before had a girl washed ashore in a Lost Boat. He must've sensed the boat's arrival, a slight tremor in the Island that sent him to investigate. He'd expected a new Lost Boy, no doubt. He would've never suspected a girl, especially not now.

Nevertheless, he pulled a dimpled grin as he approached the boat. "Welcome to Neverland."

She turned convincingly scared eyes up at him. Her frail form shivered for good measure.

Please believe it, she silently prayed. *Take the bait.*

The boy extended his hand, the wind tugging at his messy hair. "Don't be afraid. You're safe now."

Her stomach clenched suspiciously. She knew what he'd meant, but she was anything but safe. Nothing about what she was getting herself into was safe.

Finally, she put her small hand in his and allowed him to help her out of the boat. His hand was warm, rough, the kind of hands you'd want your protector to have. The kind of hands you didn't want for your enemy.

"I'm Peter," Pan introduced himself, she already knew exactly who he was. "Who are you?"

"Jane," she said weakly, the better to hide the sharp edge in her voice. "My name is Jane."

CHAPTER TWO
NEVERPEAK

Wendy Darling knew instantly when the ticking stopped and colors washed away. There was something in the air, something in the way her head leapt and stomach flopped. Her whole being knew she was back in Neverland before her brain could register it or eyes comprehend it.

There was the jungle stretching far below them, and Crocodile Creek cutting through vast and rushing. Greyish blue touched crisp azure as the shifting seas met the sky on the horizon. She could hear the crashing waterfall that fed the Creek somewhere below amongst the green mountains. If she turned and looked hard enough, perhaps she would make out the Panther Tribe's camp atop the cliffs of Flying Eagle Peninsula; or look the other way to find the mirror waters of Mermaid Lagoon.

Home, Wendy thought happily. *I'm home.*

Kai Ødegård walked over to her side. "So, this is Neverland."

"It's beautiful," Rubina Daim commented.

Jack Caldwell breathed in deeply through his nose. "The air is fresh!"

"Are you saying Wonderland's air wasn't?" Alice Liddell questioned, arching her eyebrows dangerously.

"No, what I meant was that there isn't a mome rath around every corner," Jack clarified before adding under his breath, "or a certain rabbit for that matter."

Red elbowed him in the ribs, but Jack only smiled.

Wendy's brow furrowed. *Wait a moment...*

She looked around them, at the view, at the tip of...
Her face paled. "Neverpeak," she muttered.

"What is it?" Alice voiced concern.

Before Wendy could answer, a tremor ran down the mountain where they stood. The ground shook, nearly causing them to lose their balance. She turned to look at the top of Neverpeak Mountain. The tip seemed so close. But it wasn't the mountain itself that terrified her. It was the creature that inhabited it.

"Kyta."

"Who or, better yet, *what* is that?" Jack questioned as the mountain shook again.

An ear splitting cry pierced through the sky. It jabbed through her bones like a knife, sending paranoid chills down her spine. The five froze stalk still.

Wendy's eyes widened as she searched for where the cry came from, or better yet, where they could easily escape to. "She's the dragon of Neverpeak Mountain."

Alice gulped. "Didn't you tell me that the dragon doesn't like intruders?"

"Yep. And we're on her mountain."

Another cry split the air, louder, closer. Twisting around the mountain side and through the trees emerged a scaly dragon head. Kyta was slender, making her nimble as she moved between the trees. Her scales were pale green in the shadows, but turned pearly white in the sunlight. She loomed over them in graceful and horrific beauty, her reptilian eyes glaring.

"I'm thinking we look a lot like intruders," Kai growled.

"What do we do?" Red asked. "Do we fight it; kill it?"

Wendy shook her head. "You can't kill Kyta. It's not possible."

"Well, I don't fancy being a dragon's next snack," Jack said. "So, what do you suggest we do?"

She nodded to the side where the mountain didn't drop in a cliff. "Run."

*****

"Gosh, Jane." Peter grinned. "You're a natural!"

Jane swung her sword to clash against his. "Thanks."

Their cutlasses crashed together as the two dueled. Pan was training her to use a sword, or that's what she led him to believe. Of course, she had to play it down a notch so as not to give herself away.

These last few days had been good for her. Jane's hair was the short and glossy black as it normally was. Her stomach had been well fed and she no longer looked as bony as she did when she arrived in the stolen Lost Boat. The Lost Boys had accepted her as one of their own.

They didn't suspect a thing.

"GO, JANE!" the spectating Lost Boys cried.

"Yeah, kick his butt!" a younger boy encouraged.

Unfortunately, she thought to herself, *I can't do that just yet.*

She swung her blade at him. Jane knew what the result would be, but she made it look like a rookie mistake. Peter easily backed up and quickly knocked the sword out of her grasp. Jane raised her hands in defeat as Pan held his sword to her throat.

The Lost Boys cheered. Peter grinned, dropping his sword to his side. He held out his hand in a friendly gesture. Jane pulled a smile as she shook it, no longer feeling the urge to pull it away so quickly.

"Nice job, Jane," Pan commented. "We'll make a Lost Girl out of you, yet."

He grinned. It was the first time she noticed it: his teeth. Weren't they supposed to be baby teeth? The gnashing little pearls that all the legends said he had? But Pan didn't have a single baby tooth in his mouth. They were all normal; long on top, a bit jumbled on the bottom.

When did Peter Pan start to grow up?

*****

The trees whizzed by as Wendy ran down the mountain, the others at her heals. Kyta bounded after them, smoke blowing from her nostrils. No one stopped or faltered in pace. The only thought in their minds was that they needed to get off of that mountain.

Jack slipped and fell on his back, the loose dirt dragging him into a landslide down the mountain slope.

"Whoa!" he cried as he struggled to stop.

Red skidded to a halt. "JACK!"

"I'm fine," Jack called up as he slid down in a cloud of dirt. "Keep going!"

She didn't move until the landslide ended and Jack was back on his feet. Coughing up dust, Jack waved Red on and staggered into a run once more.

When Wendy finally reached level ground, she stopped. Bending over, she placed her hands on her knees as she caught her breath. She couldn't hear Kyta anymore. The dragon probably flew off to her cave once she found that the intruders were retreating from her mountain. Wendy knew this was the case. She sensed it in the air, felt it in the ground. Peter taught her long ago how to read the Island and listen when it spoke to her. Kyta was back in her cave. They were safe.

"It's alright!" Wendy called at last, straightening. "Kyta went back to her cave. We're, we're... safe."

She looked around. The jungle surrounded her, but she was alone.

Where did they go? she wondered.

But the Island wouldn't disclose that to her.

Panic rose in her abdomen. They must've gotten separated sometime during their escape. Wendy felt overtaken with worry. She was the only one who knew the Island's secrets, where to go, what dangers to look out for. Without her help... Who knew what kind of trouble her friends could get into?

CHAPTER THREE
SEPARATED

Kai leaped over a fallen log, a lone fox skittering out of the way. He landed wrong on his bad leg and as pain split up his shin, he tumbled over, rolling down the steep hill and barely missing the trees in his way.

The world stopped spinning suddenly as he landed hard on his back, the breath knocked out of him. Gasping, he waited for his heart to steady, for the dark spots in his vision to retreat. He mentally checked himself for any injuries other than the aching bruises all over and the increasingly massive headache. Concluding nothing serious, he eased himself up.

As he struggled to his feet, pain shot down his bone in his right leg. He groaned, cursing under his breath. Unfortunately, despite the White Queen's healing back in Wonderland, that bad landing must've done it in. Kai could only manage a slight limp when he walked.

He rubbed the back of his head where a growing bump throbbed, looking up the steep slope he'd tumbled down. There was no use climbing back up the mountain. Wendy had said the dragon didn't like intruders, and Kai didn't want to test the scaly beast.

Kai looked around the jungle that surrounded him, not a recognizable landmark in sight. "Where am I?"

*****

"ALICE!" Wendy shouted as loud as she could, "RED! JACK! KAI! WHERE ARE YOU?"

"WENDY!"

Her head turned sharply to the sound of her name. "Red?"

● ● ●

"WENDY!" Red's voice was closer that time.

"OVER HERE!"

Red emerged from the bushes, twigs clinging to her black hair. Wendy sighed in relief, rushing up to her friend. She was shocked when Red pulled her into a hug.

"Wendy; thank heavens," Red gasped, pulling away. "I can't find anyone else! I can't sense them, I can't hear them, I can't smell them..."

"I know! I don't know where..." Wendy stopped, Red's words suddenly dawning on her. "Wait, what do you mean?"

Red grasped her shoulders. "Wendy, the Island, it's keeping it in!"

"The Island's keeping *what* in?"

Her green eyes were wide and frightened, more frightened than she'd ever seen them. "Neverland's preventing the Wolf from coming out. It's keeping the Wolf trapped inside me!"

"So, you're... you're not a wolf anymore; at least not here?" Wendy questioned, confused. "But, that's not too bad at all. I don't see what's wrong."

"It's not like I'm left defenseless," Red admitted. "But now, I won't be able to sense danger approaching, not like before. And I won't be able to track the others down, either."

Wendy's heart fell a little. "So, we're on our own. No short cuts."

Red nodded.

Just like old times then, Wendy thought, deciding not to dwell on this as too much of a negative. She'd survived in Neverland for decades without a Wolf friend before. But then she'd had Peter and the Lost Boys on her side. Now they didn't even know she was back in Neverland.

"But what about you?" Red cut through her thoughts. "You're back in Neverland. Can't you, you know, fly?"

Fly?

That was a good question. For a moment, she almost considered the possibility. But she knew that was impossible. She might be in Neverland, she may even see Peter, but until she got her happy thoughts back, flying was not an option.

"I can't," Wendy explained. "I need to find my happy thought. I left it in Hangman's Tree, so I suppose..." Her voice trailed off as her gaze wandered to the forestry around them.

Something's not right.

The leaves were browning and brittle, the bark peeling off the tree trunks. The grass underfoot was yellow and dry. Wendy took a twig from Red's hair, examining it worriedly.

"What is it?" Red asked.

Wendy snapped the twig in half. "It's dead."

"Well, of course it's dead! It's a twig."

"No, not the twig," she mumbled. "The Island, it's... sad."

Red furrowed her eyebrows. "Sad?"

"...Depressed."

A dull purpose settled over her. Wendy turned away and walked into the jungle, still holding the two halves of twig in hand. She heard Red hastily followed her.

We need to find Peter.

"How can the Island be depressed?" Red broke through her ponderings.

"Peter and the Island are linked," Wendy explained while walking. "The Island reflects Peter's general emotions. If he's sick, the Island acts like it's sick. If he's happy, the Island is lush and beautiful."

"So, if the Island is depressed…" Red wacked away a low hanging branch that wanted to tangled in her long hair.

"Then Peter is, too."

Spitting out leaves, Red asked, "But, what happens to Neverland if Peter… dies?"

Wendy stopped abruptly, heart skipping a beat. Her fingers released the twig's broken pieces at last. Red lowered her eyes guiltily.

But she still answered with hardly a quiver, "Then the Island will select a new Pan. It will pick someone else to care for the Lost Boys and the Island."

Biting her lip, Wendy chose a spot on the ground to kneel. She began drawing in the dirt, trying to figure out where they needed to go. Red stood by, watching as the map took shape.

"We'll have to go to Hangman's Tree, of course," Wendy muttered. "Once we find Peter, he'll help us find the others."

Red hissed something, but she didn't catch it. Perhaps she was just imagining.

"We'll have to keep an eye out for them, in case we find them before getting there," Wendy continued talking to herself, wishing she'd told the others more about the Island before. "And of course we'll have to keep an ear out for any sign of this ultimate terror we need to figure out. I wonder who this *Master* is, anyway. Maybe it's Hook?"

"Wendy," Red spoke harsher.

"What?"

"I think someone's watching us," she whispered.

Her stomach felt hollow then. Looking around, Wendy stood slowly, regretting she let her guard down. A faint rustle in the trees turned her head.

Ten bodies fell from the treetops surrounding them, bows drawn and arrows aimed. Each were clad in animal skins, and most had tattoos on their arms. Their faces were adorned with paint strokes.

Wendy almost cursed, but she held her tongue. She raised her hands in surrender, eyeing Red as she reluctantly followed suit. One of the tribesmen lowered his bow and approached them. As he tied their hands together, the tribesmen talked amongst themselves in their own language.

Wendy only understood a portion of what they said, but it was enough.

"What are they saying, Wendy?" Red asked as the tribesmen began to pull them along like prisoners. "Where are they taking us?"

"They're taking us to Tiger Lily."

*****

"Hello?!" Jack called. "Where'd everybody go?"

He looked around the trees, searching for the others. A squirrel skittered away, chattering angrily at him. Jack slapped aside a tree branch only to have it snap back and hit him in the nose. His face smarting, he broke the branch off in frustration.

"Red? Wendy? Alice? Kai? *Agh!*" Jack slapped his neck, killing the mosquito that had bitten him. "Blasted bug."

A loud growl echoed through the jungle, followed by bird cries. Jack froze in his tracks, breath caught in his throat. An eerie howl sounded. A chill went down his spine.

"Uh, Red? Is that you?"

But something told him it wasn't Red. He continued on cautiously through the jungle.

"Alright guys, this isn't funny," Jack persisted. "You can come out now. Joke's on me."

But there was no response. Wendy didn't come out laughing. Kai didn't step out from behind the next tree. Alice didn't slink out of the bushes. And Red didn't jump up on him, smiling, to tell him everything was alright.

Jack was all alone with nothing but a broken branch in hand.

*****

Alice got a face full of dry, dead leaves. She wacked them out of her eyes and spat them out of her mouth as she ran on. She dared not look back.

Alice broke through the underbrush and came to an abrupt halt as her breath caught. A bear stared at her with beady black eyes, sitting back on its haunches. Its nose twitched to identify her scent. A vacant beehive lay broken open at its feet.

Upon seeing Alice, the bear got down on all fours and stood over its meal. Terror seized her as the bear glared at her. She backed away slowly, trying not to make any sudden movements. The bear opened its maw, its teeth yellow. Drool and honey dribbled from its lips. The bear growled menacingly, making Alice jump.

She turned quickly and ran as fast as her legs could carry her.

CHAPTER FOUR
CAPTAIN JAMES HOOK

He twisted at his mustache between his fingers, deep in thought. Sea blue eyes observed the map of Neverland on his desk, plans and fantasies running through his muddled brain. A double cigar holder was clenched in his teeth. Two wisps of smoke curled out of the ends. The locks that fell over his shoulders had a few strands of grey amongst the oil black.

His fine coat was strangely scarlet, not a shade expected of a pirate to wear. But the garment had been made for him by someone he cared very much about. And if inspected closely, the coat would show that it was not so fine as it appeared. There were places where the fabric was almost worn through, where the color had faded with age. In some spots, badly sewn stitches where holes came through had been hastily, frantically sewn together. It was a bit snug in some places where the fabric had shrunk and there was a gold button missing. But he still wore it like it was the finest treasure he had, and he'd never dare part with it.

His steely gaze ventured to the iron claw attached to the metal cuff permanently bound about his wrist. What pain it had been when the blacksmith seared the metal to the stump where his hand used to be. But he bore it all the same. Besides, at the time there was a much worse pain inside him that even the burn of hot metal could not overwhelm. And when asked if he wanted to attach anything to replace his hand, he could've asked for anything. He could've had a sword, a steel hand, a bottle of rum, anything really. It surprised everyone when he insisted upon the iron hook, the very item that became the symbol of his sworn revenge.

Ah, revenge; that was what he wanted. It was a craving, a longing, a thirst that he'd been deprived of for too long. It became his life's only purpose. It was the only thing he desired, the only thing he lived for. He convinced himself that revenge was the only thing that would bring him peace. He couldn't rest until he had it in his grasp. Revenge overwhelmed him, taken hold of his whole being. Nothing could stop it.

He could almost taste the sweetness of revenge as he felt it come closer. It was there, brushing his fingertips, tickling his nose, teasing his soul. It's what he dreamed of night after night, what he thought of day after day. Revenge had become such a necessity to him that it had become his weakness. He would do anything, sacrifice anything, and work for anyone if it meant executing his revenge.

He was a different man because of revenge. He knew it deep down in his black heart, but he didn't care. To him, it made him a better pirate. It made him stronger than before, more ruthless and bloodthirsty. It made him respected and feared. No one dared disobey or question him and his authority. He'd become the most feared and dangerous pirate in the whole of Blind Man's Bluff; so much so that the very name of Captain James Hook brought terror to the scene.

What he didn't know about his thirst for revenge was that though it made him a stronger pirate, it also made him a weaker man. It ate away at him from the inside out, taking over his soul. His conscience barely existed, having been devoured by revenge. The love he used to have had long since died away, leaving only a shadow that could be easily manipulated by revenge. There was more monster than man in him because of it.

Only one thing kept him from being completely taken over by revenge, one person. It took everything within him not to forget that.

CHAPTER FIVE
TRIBESMEN GRUDGE

Wendy received a sharp kick in the ribs and jerked awake instantly. A stern face glared down at her; gave a low grunt. *So hostile,* Wendy thought begrudgingly. Whatever happened to the times when Lost Boys and Panther Tribesmen were allies?

I suppose those never lasted long anyway. It's all just a game until somebody decides to switch sides.

Before Red could receive a similar wakening, Wendy wiggled over to her. "Red," she whispered, nudging her gently. "Wake up."

Red's eyes snapped open so fast Wendy saw her pupils constrict and dilate when exposed to the dim light. She sat up slowly, stiffly.

"It's time to go," Wendy explained softly.

"Oh joy," Red groaned as they struggled to their feet. "I'm starting to *really* look forward to meeting this Tiger Lily."

A tribeswoman with feathers strung through her braid came up to make sure their bounds were still tight. After tightening the loose ropes, she gave them each a handful of nuts before they were dragged along behind the tribesmen band. Wendy popped the nuts in her mouth, afraid of dropping them, but chewed slowly. She couldn't help but notice their captors had kept some berries to themselves.

The long trek gave her enough time to properly mull over her worries. Where were the others: Alice, Kai, Jack? Were they alright? What if they were to run into Panther Tribesmen as well? The tribe didn't always take prisoners...

She shuddered at the thought of her friends lying cold on the jungle floor; their empty eyes, blood soaked bodies, arrows flowering from their chests.

No, stop that! Wendy shoved the picture from her mind. Curse her overactive imagination.

Still, the scenarios continued to come one after another.

What if they stumbled upon Mermaid Lagoon? Alice might be alright; the mermaids' powers didn't work on girls. But if Jack or Kai fell prey to their enchantments, if they didn't know better, then either one could walk into the trap. Mermaids, as she understood, could be unbearably persuasive.

Then there were the pirates. Those merciless brutes almost *never* took captives. And if her friends were alone... Wendy shivered. The pirates typically traveled in groups, occasionally pairs. If Jack, Alice, or Kai encountered a pack of bloodthirsty pirates, the boys would most likely be murdered and Alice would be ruthlessly taken to Blind Man's Bluff.

Wendy's palms grew sweaty. The nuts were getting harder to swallow.

The jungle was full of beasts: tigers, bears, coyotes; any could easily kill an unsuspecting stranger to the Island. The Crocodile was always up for a snack. And who's to say the others hadn't escaped the dragon?

No, they had to have at least made it off the mountain, Wendy assured herself. *They had to.*

Then it dawned on her. What if her friends ran into the Lost Boys? They could get the wrong idea, maybe think that Alice, Jack, and Kai were pirates or tribesmen. Not that any of them could pass for a tribesman. Even so, judging by the way the tribe was treating her, Wendy assumed that the Lost Boys weren't on good terms with them anyway. As much as she wanted to believe that the others could find safety with them, the Lost Boys had no clue she was back, not to mention she'd brought friends...

Something jabbed her in the back, snapping her out of her stupor. Wendy quickened her lagging pace before looking back to find one of the tribeswomen had hit her with the flat end of her spear.

"Hey!" Red barked angrily in Wendy's defense.

She noticed the pity in the tribeswoman's eyes briefly before they glazed over, harsh and unyielding. Wendy understood. Panther Tribesmen had souls, too, after all. But in Neverland, being hard was an easy defense mechanism to survive. It could be so difficult to stay soft in such a place where it was unclear whether dreams or nightmares would come true.

Wendy should know.

She'd been battling it for decades.

*****

Alice burst from the thicket, completely lost and undoubtable terrified. She hadn't gotten a wink of sleep the previous night. The sounds of the jungle kept her awake all night long. And after seeing far too many questionable shadows, she dared not rest for more than a moment. She could've traveled halfway around the island by now for all she knew. That's how her legs felt, anyway.

The sky broke loose and rain drizzled down. Alice blinked it out of her eyes, water running down her face and hair hanging in wet strands. The ground was slick, and soon she was soaked to her knees in mud.

Were those footsteps behind her? She quickened her pace to a jog, afraid to run lest she'd fall, afraid to walk lest something catch her. Her feet sloshed with every step. Completely drenched by now, her hair stuck agitatedly to her face. She developed the habit of constantly checking her neck to make sure the chain hadn't slipped off and the pocket watch still hung by her heart. That was their one ticket home. She could not lose it.

Her foot hit a slick spot and she pitched forward, falling hard on the ground. Exhaustion grabbed her, letting her head lay there despite the side of her face being in mud. The rain fell continuously on her back. Alice just lay there watching the raindrops shatter on the ground.

You need to keep going, Alice, her common sense prodded, but she was much too tired.

Time stretched to an inconceivable expanse. Sleep only came as a daze if it ever came at all. Alice's senses dulled until she hardly felt the chill in her bones, heard the rain pattering, or saw the dense jungle scene around her.

The whisper of bells brushed past her ear. Alice lifted a heavy head and looked up. Perhaps it was simply her mind playing tricks on her, but a twinkle of light winked in the dark jungle before disappearing.

Alice hastily pushed herself up. The rain was only dripping. But she hardly felt the raindrops anymore. She was already soaked to the skin. Wiping the muck off of her face with the back of her hand, her boots squishing in mud, Alice stumbled forward. She didn't know where she aimed to go, but something guided her in the direction of where the light might have been. Bells still rang softly in the distance, or perhaps from the back of her own mind.

But perhaps the bells weren't even bells at all…

She quickened her pace, eagerness kindling.

Her rapid pace cut short abruptly. A rock formation blocked her path, it's ledge too high to see in the dim light. Leafy vines draped over the wet stone like a curtain. Alice's heart dropped in disappointment.

Wendy had once told her of Neverland and its inhabitants. It felt like ages ago when she'd first met Wendy and the others back at the Facility. How long ago was that; two or maybe three months since Alice arrived there under her father's orders? Not as long as she'd thought.

Alice had felt certain she'd made it to the one place where she would be safe on the Island. The bells seemed louder and the air tingled, but maybe it was just the effects of the rain and lack of sleep. The giant rock wall swelled before her mockingly. But if there was one thing Alice learned in Wonderland, it was that things were not always as they seemed.

She reached up for the hanging vines. They rippled at her touch as if dancing. But her fingers didn't feel the cold stone behind those vines.

Hope surging once more, Alice pushed aside the curtain where darkness swam before her. She entered the cave for shelter if nothing else. She hadn't realized how wet she was until out of the rain. Hugging herself, a shiver went down her spine. Inside, it was not as dark as she'd thought. Water fell from her hair and splatted the ground, but it didn't echo. *Strange.* She rubbed her wet shoulders in a poor attempt to warm up.

Venturing deeper into the tunnel, an eerie shadow hung over what she assumed was the exit. Dim light filtered through.

More vines, she thought curiously.

Alice pushed aside the leafy tentacles and stepped out.

*****

"So, what happened between you and Tiger Lily, anyway?" Red asked.

What a question, Wendy laughed to herself.

"It's... complicated," she admitted at last. "I suppose it started because... Or rather is the result of... Well, let's just say Tiger Lily doesn't like to let go of a grudge."

She winced when she received a poke in the back with a spear. Silently, she scolded herself for it. She should've known better than to talk about the Panther Tribe's Princess like that. Even if their captors didn't know exactly what she said, they could still hear the bitterness in her tone. Well, not exactly bitterness. But she supposed it was too complicated to describe it as anything else.

Red snuck a glare at the man who struck Wendy. "What do you mean?"

Learning from her mistake, she kept her tone steady, "Tiger Lily's father, the Panther Tribe's Chief wanted to combine forces with the Lost Boys to defeat the pirates. Of course, he was thinking more of a *permanent* alliance." She suppressed a laugh at the thought. "He wanted to bind Peter and Tiger Lily in marriage, bringing together the tribe and the boys."

Red tripped on a tree root. Wendy snatched her arm before she could fall, supporting her until Red regained her footing.

"I wouldn't say Tiger Lily was exactly excited about this plan of engagement," she continued, "but she saw the benefits and deemed it best for the tribe. Peter didn't know of these plans, of course. It was just an idea that could've had potential. But, then—"

"Then you came along," Red guessed.

Wendy shrugged. "Tiger Lily never really *loved* Peter. She just, I don't know, laid claim to him. She respected him as a great leader, a brave warrior, and a kind person. I suppose she mistook that respect for love. So when I came to Neverland, Tiger Lily saw me as a threat. She hated me before she met me. It didn't help much that I almost left her to the mercy of the mermaids on our first meeting…"

"You *what?*"

"Don't give me that; it was a long time ago! I was rather… frazzled at the time with Peter having a moment of complete arrogance. In the end, I'm the one who reminded that stupid boy that Tiger Lily was drowning." Wendy chuckled at the memory, so distant yet still there. "Anyway, when it was clear that I kept coming back to Neverland, her peacefulness toward the Lost Boys turned prickly. She's held a grudge against me ever since."

One of the men barked something that sounded a lot like a rude way to say *quiet*. A woman with a bear claw through her earlobe gave him and earful of criticism. He looked sheepishly at her, hanging his head as if her tongue were a whip. Red raised an eyebrow, but Wendy smiled.

By late afternoon, after a long walk with no rest or disruptions, they came upon a landmark Wendy knew well.

A great gulch cut into the landscape before them. Tall rock walls bordered the valley below, a sheer drop from where they stood. Clusters of trees were scattered throughout the inside of the gulch. A gorgeous waterfall on the far side fell into a twisting river at the ravine's bottom.

The tribesmen dubbed this the spot to rest.

"Slightly Gulch," Wendy muttered, sitting closer to the edge than the others.

Red nibbled on course bread. "That thing doesn't look *slightly* anything."

Wendy shook her head humorously. "No, Slightly is one of the Lost Boys. The gulch is named after him."

"Why?" Red asked, handing over the canteen of water being passed around.

Wendy took a drink before explaining, "I don't know exactly. Some say there was a war held down in the gulch and Slightly led the Lost Boys to victory. Others say that's where Slightly's Lost Boat—the ones that pick up boys from the Mainland—ended up in that river down there. Still others say that he simply appeared down there."

"What do you think happened?"

"Well, Slightly is one that's been with Peter the longest. It's highly possible that Slightly was the one who spread all the rumors about it. He probably named the gulch after himself and Peter just went along with it as a kind of joke."

She didn't voice the possibility that there may be a more significant reason why it was named Slightly Gulch, but that it was long forgotten. No one ever liked to admit

• • •

how the Island seeped away your memory the longer you stayed or the younger you were. Wendy had gone back and forth between the Mainland and Neverland for decades. How many memories blurred or even disappeared in that time? The scary thing was, there was no real way of knowing.

Red couldn't help but laugh. "That sounds like something Jack would do."

Wendy smiled. "It certainly does."

She looked out over Slightly Gulch. Her gut filled with such longing it ached. The map in her head told her that Hangman's Tree was just beyond that waterfall; perhaps half a day's journey if they headed a bit northeast. If it wasn't for the tribesmen, Wendy and Red might've made it there by nightfall. But they weren't going that way.

Wendy sighed. *So close and yet so far.*

The group spent the rest of the day walking continuously. They left Slightly Gulch far behind them. They traveled unfailingly west, always west.

Wendy observed in dismay as the jungle slowly blended into the forest that inhabited the Flying Eagle Peninsula. She knew their destination was becoming closer and closer with each footstep. The sound of the sea clashed on either side of them as waves threw themselves against the cliffs. An eagle's shriek split through the blue sky. A majestic bald eagle flew side by side with a beautiful black eagle. Wendy once pondered how many different eagles could be on one island. But she pondered different things now.

As they walked on, Wendy noticed how their numbers grew as Panther Tribe's hunters slipped out of the bushes or dropped from the trees. It was as if they simply appeared, gradually, silently. But she was familiar with their methods, their talent for lurking undetected through the jungle. Even the animals that accompanied some seemed to adapt the shadowy silence. A golden eagle sat contently on its master's arm, a white bellied sea eagle waiting quietly on a woman's shoulder. The dogs that trotted along had a particular interest in Red, sniffing her feet and lingering around her. A dingo even went so far as to lick her fingers. Wendy wondered if they sensed the Wolf in Red.

Her heart leapt when the forest broke into a clearing. The high grounds were exposed on all sides, but the sheer drop to the sea provided assurance of no invasion, and the stretch of clearing would insure no surprise attacks from the one end the tribesmen kept guard on. But the sight of the Panther Tribe's camp brought back such nostalgia that she didn't feel the dread she initially expected.

Still, Wendy hoped Tiger Lily wouldn't try to kill her again.

CHAPTER SIX
THE JUNGLE

Jack jumped down from the tree and landed louder than intended. When shins eased from the jarring drop, he picked up his broken branch and walked off. Though he regretted not bringing a sword from Wonderland, at least the staff would serve as a decent weapon. Unfortunately, it also reminded him of a weapon he'd carried in Giant Country. Shoving away the bad memories, he focused on more important matters: food.

His stomach growled. Jack hadn't eaten anything since yesterday. If he was going to wander this bloody island for long, he needed to fill his annoyingly empty stomach. There was no use trying to find his friends if he was too weak with hunger to carry on his search.

Using his oversized stick, he swatted aside a giant spider web in his path. He twitched every time something brushed his neck, hoping it wasn't a homeless spider seeking revenge.

An eerie howl sent icy fingers down his spine. Jack's heart skipped a beat.

Red.

He turned on his heal towards the direction of the howl and ran through the jungle. Hope surged through him. If he found Red, then they could easily find the others, what with her strong sense of smell.

Jack wouldn't have to wander Neverland alone after all.

*****

Kai tried to stay as still as possible. His back pressed against the trunk of a sturdy tree and his sore leg stretched out on the limb he sat on. Using his right leg to help support him, he looked down from his perch three meters above the ground, waiting. Thankfully, the jungle was so dense that no one would see him up in the tree.

The waiting was long and tiresome, but he was used to it. Kai knew he couldn't go aimlessly about Neverland with a bad leg. He needed direction.

Somehow, he had to get to Hangman's Tree. Once there, all he had to do was convince Pan that they needed to search the Island for Wendy, Red, Jack, and Alice. Hopefully Pan would believe him. Unfortunately, Kai knew he wouldn't have the most convincing story. But perhaps if he told the Lost Boys everything he knew about Wendy, then that would prove him true.

At least he hoped so.

He had no other choice.

First he had to get there. Thus, his reasonable conclusion: He'd have to stop and ask for directions. Theoretically.

I'll have to be persuasive, Kai reasoned.

It'd be best if he found a Lost Boy.

There was only one problem with his plan. No one came to the spot he was lurking.

Kai kept his eyes trained on the area below. He didn't want to miss his opportunity if and when it arose. Though the jungle was alive with noise, his hearing remained on edge for anything unusual. He tried to keep his mind focused, stay alert, not let his thoughts wander. Because every time they did, the memories came flooding back.

• • •

Gerda with her sweet smile came up in his mind's eye, reminding him of all the happy memories before all of *this*.

But then her face melted away and the fight with the Snow Queen replaced it. The bitter cold seethed into his bones, making it harder and harder to move. The flash of light, and pain like fire shot through his whole body, nearly reaching his very soul. Glass and ice shattered, fragments flying in all directions. And then a scream so desperate pierced through the pain: Gerda. The spell that would've killed him stopped suddenly. He found himself staring into Gerda's teary eyes as he fell out of that world.

Kai jerked awake, his hand flying to his scar on his jaw. Ice daggers of pain shot down it just as it had when he'd received it. Cold sweat soaked his skin. His body shivered in the memory's freezing shadow. The pain disintegrated, but his fingers continued tracing the scar running down his jaw bone.

Kai took heavy breaths, trying not to fall off the branch he sat on. How long had he been asleep? He looked up at the sky to see the sun directly overhead.

Great, he thought irritatingly, *a whole morning gone.*

He looked down from his perch once more and held his breath. A man lumbered out of the undergrowth, his forehead high and eyebrows thick. A nose the size of small potato sat over a black toothed sneer. He wore a single gold hoop through one ear. His broad arms were hairy; uneven stubble grew on his chin. No doubt, he was a pirate.

Kai noted the cutlass strapped to the pirate's belt, the glint of a knife hidden in his boot. The way his eyes wandered suggested he was looking for something. It didn't look as though the pirate was staying for long.

Kai cautiously readied himself, wishing it'd been a Lost Boy, deciding he'd have to make due. With that thought in mind, he jumped.

He landed smoothly enough, tucking and rolling as soon as he hit the ground. The pirate was in such shock, he didn't counter as Kai jumped to his feet and snatched the knife from his boot. Coming to his senses, the pirate threw a punch at him, but Kai instinctively ducked out of the way and slammed into the pirate's stomach with full force. He rammed into a nearby tree, pinned there by Kai's strong arm. He held a knife to the pirate's throat.

"Which way to Hangman's Tree?" Kai growled.

"Ye're not a Lost Boy, eh?" The pirate smirked. "Figures; ye're a little old to be one."

Kai pressed the blade against the man's throat, skin stretching. "Just answer the question."

"Ye accent's funny... Ye can't get in Hangman's Tree if ye ain't a Lost Boy or a bloody Panther. Dangerous business trying."

"I'll take my chances," Kai insisted, drawing a thin line of blood that trickled down the pirate's throat.

The pirate pointed east, a cruel grin spreading to revealing black teeth.

"Good luck," he croaked.

Kai looked from the jungle to the pirate. "If I find out you lied to me, I will personally hunt you down and make you regret it."

Using the knife's hilt, he hit the pirate over the head with enough strength to knock him unconscious.

• • •

Kai removed the sheath from the pirate's boot, attaching it to his own belt and sheathing the knife. Perhaps he should take the cutlass, too, but then he thought about walking into Hangman's Tree fully armed. That wouldn't go over well with the Lost Boys. But he couldn't leave the pirate with a weapon, either. So Kai grabbed the sword and threw it into the underbrush deep in the jungle. There was a chance the pirate would find it when he awoke, but Kai would be long gone by then.

With his new weapon, Kai headed east, away from the slowly setting sun.

*****

Jack walked on through the jungle, disgruntled. There was no Red, no clue where his friends were, no idea where on this bloody island he was. On top of it all, there was no food. He walked aimlessly, grouchily, his staff dragging the ground beside him.

He trudged through a patch of leafy overgrowth. Swatting aside greenery, sharp points pricked his hand. Jerking back, Jack hissed in shock and pain. He tried his best to pick out the thorns in his palm, but some were just too tiny for him to remove. Making a mental note to ask one of the girls remove them when he found them, Jack searched for the thing that hurt him.

He quickly found what he was looking for. A long blackberry vine was entangled in the bushes' leafy cluster. Something clicked in his mind: Where there were blackberry vines, there were bound to be blackberries. Hastily, Jack followed the thorny vine until he found the end.

Jack cursed, turning around to find the vine's source instead of its tip. Just his luck, the vine was brittle and snapped at the next turn. It took him a while to find the rest of the vine again.

After twisting around trees and shuffling through bushes, Jack found the largest patch of blackberries he had ever seen. Though, that wasn't saying much seeing as he hadn't seen too many blackberry bushes. It didn't take long for him to start gulfing down the juicy berries. Some of were sour and not yet ripe, but he didn't really care. His belly was happy, though his tongue complained.

A low growl rumbled behind him, freezing his hand on the path to drop berries in his mouth. A lump formed in his throat. The growl rumbled again. Turning around, Jack discovered the pair of yellow eyes watching him. He dropped the berries as he raised his arms out as if to steady the large female cougar.

"Whoa!" Jack tried to stay the big cat. "Stay back, kitty."

The cougar narrowed her eyes.

"Please?"

She yowled the kind of scream only cougars could cry, extending her paw as if to whack him aside.

Jack backed up hastily. "Hold it; let's not be hasty with tearing me to shreds. You want the berries?"

Her lips pulled back in a snarl and she hissed.

Jack gulped. "I'll take that as a yes."

The cougar stalked closer, fangs bared. Jack backed away slowly, wishing the cat would stop looking at him like he was a tasty snack. The cougar cried again, making him jump against his will.

"You know what, the berries are all yours!" Jack stammered. "I'll just, uh… I'll just be going now."

In a flash, Jack turned on his heal to go, hesitated, then turned back to grab his branch before sprinting off into the jungle once more. The cougar screamed again for good measure before climbing up a nearby tree to take an afternoon nap.

*****

A victorious crow filled the air as Pan led a group of Lost Boys into Hangman's Tree. A flood of boys took up the excited cry as they met their leader to see what the hunting party brought back with them. Some swung down from the tree houses on ropes while others popped up from underground tunnels.

Jane turned toward the scene and hastened to catch the group before it became too crowded. In the chaotic excitement, she ran right into the person she'd wanted to meet.

"Whoa, slow down there." Pan laughed. "What's the rush, Jane?"

She blinked, caught off guard.

Blast it, Jane! Think of something!

"Oh, well… I just wanted to know what you came back with," she lied.

Pan raised an eyebrow. "Oh, that? The Twins heard rumor of a beast even Tiger Lily's puss couldn't catch. And, well," he gestured back to the group, "we just caught it."

Several boys were struggling to lug an enormous tiger decorated in scars into camp. Jane suppressed her scowl at the sight.

Do they just hunt such creatures for fun? she thought in disdain. *No wonder the tribesmen don't get along well with the Lost Boys.*

But she knew that the pirates were even worse about killing for the enjoyment of it.

"The new boy killed it," Pan went on as the Twins hoisted a kid with dark hair over his eyes up on their shoulders. "It's a shame, but honestly, it's a good thing he did. That bloodthirsty tiger has been attacking tribesmen and Lost Boys left and right. Don't know why it didn't spring on pirates, though. Probably figured it was best to leave that to the Crocodile."

Jane kept her expression solemn, though she felt slight guilt at assuming the worst of the Lost Boys. Self-defense was different from outright murder. Besides, she had no real right to judge anyway.

What am I thinking? Jane shook her head. *Quit that! Remember the mission...*

"You'll never believe how he killed it," Pan intercepted her thoughts.

"What did he use?" She guessed, sounding casual, "A spear?"

"Nope. Fire."

"He *burned* it?"

"He didn't have much choice. The tiger made a jump at one of the Twins. The new boy took a burning branch from the campfire and threw it at the beast. Lucky shot, but it distracted the tiger 'til we could kill it."

Jane raised her eyebrows, mildly fascinated. She watched the flood of Lost Boys make their way through Hangman's Tree with the slain tiger.

Pan watched on, too. "That beast will do a lot of good now. We'll use the hide for clothes, which'll be swell for the

• • •

upcoming winter. The bone will make tools and weapons. And of course the meat should make a fine feast."

"So the hunt wasn't just for the kill?"

"What? No! We try to use everything we can from the beasts we kill, like the Panther Tribe. Anything we don't use, we trade for stuff we need with Tiger Lily's gang." Pan grinned. "I'm thinking a celebration is at hand, once the Tribe hears of this. It won't be anything near a ball like Cinderella, but still."

"Cinderella?" she questioned, trying out the word. *What in the blasted world was that?*

"It's a name from a story someone told me a long time ago."

Though she was unsure why any sane person would name their child Cinderella, Jane decided to brave past her hesitation and ask, "Who?"

Pan's smile vanished; his face darkened. A cold wind swept his wild hair from his face, exposing plainly those dull, sad eyes. Jane shivered, having never seen such a drastic change on his expression before. But at the same time it seemed like he was always this way, just beneath the surface, since the time they first met. This Pan, this newly exposed layer of him, was the one she'd always feared. There was no telling what this Pan would do. And it disturbed her how easily he could conceal it.

"Excuse me," he mumbled before slinking off.

Jane almost went after him, almost wanted to apologize for reminding him of the one who was the cause of such pain and sorrow. Oh yes, she knew of the one every Lost Boy whispered about when they thought she wasn't listening. She knew who it was no one dared mention in front of Peter Pan.

Jane knew about the Bird.

She just didn't know why no one spoke of her.

Prickling sensations crawled down her neck as if she was being watched. Jane turned, searching. Amongst the chaos and celebration, there only one who didn't join the excitement.

A small boy with the appearance of a six-year-old—though Neverland was deceitful with age—stood under a treehouse in the back of the crowd. Thick black hair stuck out in every direction. He had large brown eyes and a sprinkle of freckles dotting his nose. A skunk pelt cloak hung over his shoulders, practically a perfect fit.

The boy was looking right at her.

Jane quickly turned away from his imposing gaze and grabbed the first recognizable person she found: Slightly. Appearing about fourteen, he had orange hair and mischievous eyes that struck you as someone to be cautious around lest he pick your pocket or bruise your heart. Just as when she first met him, Jane felt the urge to check the pendant around her neck to make sure it was still there. But Slightly was one of Pan's original Lost Boys, thus he was also one of the boys Pan trusted best.

Slightly gave her that crooked grin that made him look even more like an untrustworthy liar. "Hey, Jane!"

"Slightly," Jane asked, lifting her chin sideways discretely, "who's that over there?"

When he saw the boy, his smile twitched. "Who; Tootles?"

"Yeah." Jane glanced out of the corner of her eye as Tootles fell back into the shadows. "What's the matter with him?"

Slightly hesitated, eyes dropping to his feet. It was the first time he didn't have an answer for her questions, not even a cocky one.

Flustered, Jane sighed. "Fine, if you won't tell me what's wrong with Tootles, could you at least tell me what's wrong with Pan? We were talking and when I asked him a question, he completely spaced out and left."

Slightly shifted from foot to foot. "Look, Jane, I don't think…"

"How am I supposed to be a Lost Girl if you guys continue to keep secrets from me?" she shot, raising an eyebrow. The look seemed to always win over Slightly, a challenge or dare behind her eyes that she knew he couldn't resist.

Still, he looked sheepishly at her, as if reluctant to cave. "Alright, if you really must know…"

"Yes, that's what I've been trying to tell you!"

"Fine, well…" Slightly started playing with his thumbs and stealing glances at her as he rambled on, "Long time ago, Peter started making more frequent visits to the Mainland, brought back stories, seemed happier. After a while, he brought back a girl and her two brothers. He does that sometimes, you know, bringing back more Lost Boys from off the streets of the Mainland. He did that with Nibs a long time ago. Anyway, the three didn't stay too long. It was complicated since they had a family and technically they weren't *lost*. So they went home, and the brothers never did come back. But the girl…"

• • •
44

"Who was she?" Jane asked; knowing the answer before Slightly spoke but dying to hear the name of the Bird without it being whispered behind her back.

His smile twitched. "Wendy. She came back so often she practically lived here. We all liked her, Peter most of all. She lived in the treehouse you're staying at right next to Peter's; it used to be on the ground. She was as good as any Lost Boy, maybe even better in some ways. She told us stories, patched us up, admittedly saved most of our skins far more than I can count. Wendy was—" Slightly tried to suppress it, but Jane heard his voice break. "She was like a mother to most of us, a sister to others, and Peter... Well, he was closer to her than anyone."

Jane waited for him to continue, but his Adam's apple bobbed up and down as if unable to catch his voice again. "What happened to her?" she finally asked.

Slightly stared down at his twitching thumbs. "Hook killed her."

Jane felt her stomach drop and the blood drain from her face. "But how—" Now she was the one choking up, but for entirely different reasons. "How can you be sure?"

"We weren't at first," he admitted. "Peter sent his Shadow out to the Mainland to find her while we all searched the Island. We didn't find her here and his Shadow hasn't come back yet. It would've come back by now if it found her unless..."

"Unless Wendy was dead," Jane finished in a whisper.

Slightly slowly nodded. "Tootles doesn't talk much, but ever since Wendy disappeared, he's been even worse. He, well… he doesn't believe she's dead. I think he believes she'll return someday. But we all know the truth."

Jane hesitated, swallowing through her tight throat. "And Pan?"

"He tries to be hopeful, denies that she's dead, though lately he hasn't been so persistent. I think that deep down he knows the truth. He just doesn't want to accept it." Slightly added in a murmur, "None of us do."

Heavy silence wafted between them. Jane could see the discomfort and, dare she say it, *pain* in Slightly's eyes. He seemed to wait for her reaction, yet also wanted to run away. What could she say after such a story? Even she had difficulty cultivating a response.

Jane patted his arm encouragingly. "Thanks, Slightly. You can go ahead if you want. I'll catch up later."

He gave her a grateful look before skittering away like a sly fox. Jane watched him leave, wondered why he put up with her unbearable questions.

She thought about his words. *We all know the truth,* he'd said. A chill went down her spine. They didn't know the truth. They weren't even close.

But Jane knew.

She knew the truth all too well.

CHAPTER SEVEN
PIXIE HOLLOW

Alice looked around at the wonder of Pixie Hollow, marveling at how similarly it reminded her of Kensington Gardens back in London. That is, if Kensington Gardens were left ungroomed for a few years and was glittered with pixie dust. Every tree seemed to glow with their leaves' sparkling edges. Flowers looked more beautiful than any jewel. Dew drops were arranged like diamonds on grass blades.

And then, of course, there were the fairies. What magnificently darling little creatures. They only seemed to reach fourteen centimeters at the tallest, each with a pair of shiny transparent wings on their backs. When they spoke, it sounded like bells chiming behind every word and syllable.

Alice took another step into the glade, eyes wide. Instantly, she grabbed the fairies' attention. Bells jingled all around her as a flurry of pixies swarmed around her. She tried not to flinch, afraid any movement would knock the fairies from the air. But little pinches pricked her or wings tickled her when they got too close to investigate, and it was hard not to react. Most of the pixies just fluttered around her at a safe distance, a chorus of bells as they chattered among themselves.

"It's a girl!"

"There hasn't been a *girl* like this in Neverland since..."

"Perhaps she's a tribeswoman?"

"No, I've never seen a tribeswoman with such light hair."

• • •

"Jingles! She's soaked!"

"She smells like lion. Do you smell lion?"

"Rabbit, dear; it's rabbit."

"Where's that ticking coming from?"

What now? Alice thought, eyes switching from one curious face to another.

She didn't want to seem like a threat; she didn't know if they could turn hostile on her yet. Hopefully, if she played her cards right, she could get them to help her.

"Um, hello." Alice pulled an awkward smile. "I'm Alice. Pleasure to meet you and all that. Apologies about the state I'm in; it's raining outside. I can't account for the lion smell, but the rabbit I suppose would make sense, though I have no idea how that managed to stick. And, uh, no, I'm not a tribeswoman."

Too many eyes to count blinked at her, stunned. Alice wondered if she said anything wrong. Then the fairies began to titter amongst themselves, as if still unaware she could hear them.

"She can understand us!"

"Hardly anyone can understand us."

"Well, Peter can, and Tootles."

"Nibs too, but Curly can't seem to get it yet. Slightly doesn't even try!"

"Wendy could hear us, too. She didn't even need practice."

"But where did this Alice come from? What should we do?"

"We should wait for Tink."

"Tink will know what to do."

Something clicked, sending a surge of anticipation through her gut.

"Yes, Tink!" Alice exclaimed, searching for the fairy who suggested it. "That's who I need. I need to talk to Tinker Bell."

There was little Alice knew about Neverland, but if anyone could help her now, she knew Tinker Bell could.

All came to complete silence. They stared at her, and she couldn't tell if they were shocked or appalled. She felt heat crawl up her face.

One pixie flew up level to her face, the other fairies retreating to give her room. The pixie had doe brown eyes and chestnut hair pulled over her shoulder in a long braid. The deep blue dress she wore ended above her knee high leaf boots. A gold armband encircled her left bicep.

The fairy cleared her throat. "Tinker Bell isn't here right now. She's out looking for someone. We don't know when she'll be back." Her voice sounded like copper wind chimes.

Alice's shoulders slumped.

"But she's been coming back more often. She could be back soon." The fairy tried for a smile. "I'm Hazelnut, but call me Hazel. You're welcome to stay if you want."

"Thanks, I'd appreciate that."

Hazel nodded in finality before turning to her fellow fairies. "Well, everyone! We have ourselves a tired, hungry, *wet* guest. Let's fix that, shall we?"

The group of pixies hovered wide eyed for a moment before it finally registered. Jingling in agreement, fairies flew hastily in every direction.

• • •

Hazel smiled back at Alice. "Don't worry. We'll have you cleaned up in a jiffy."

Alice hoped that included some sleep.

*****

Jane looked out her window over Hangman's Tree. The boys bustled about below, doing their own thing. She watched as the Twins threw the new tiger skin over the new boy's shoulders, who ran around as if he was the great beast and pretended to scare some of the younger boys around the camp. She caught the Twins' mischievous grin as they grabbed their cutlasses and flew after the boy in the tiger skin, poking and prodding him as if teasing a beast.

That was a peculiarity Jane had tried to make sense of since she arrived there. The two were completely identical brothers with the exact same unruly blond hair that attracted twigs in the unkempt mess. Eyes were the exact same shade of pine green, the same glint of mischief. The Twins were an inseparable pair. But no one seemed to want to admit that their actual names were long forgotten. Jane was aware, of course, of how the Island ebbed away at memories. But there was hardly ever any evidence for such a claim. The fact that no one in all of Neverland could recall the Twins real names, well, it was understandably frightening to realize what kind of memories the Island could steal away.

Despite that, Jane laughed as she watched the scene. She could tell the Twins were careful not to use the cutlasses' sharp tips to draw blood or poke holes in the tiger hide. The whole thing became a fantastic game right before her eyes. Several other boys threw animal skins over their heads and ran around while others, the Twins included, pretended to hunt the *beasts*.

I wonder when I'll get my mask, Jane wondered, noting how Slightly donned the fox mask he wore when going off on expeditions, though now he used it for the game.

Which animal would I get? Something strong, to be sure. She wasn't the kind of girl to go for just any kitty mask. Still, perhaps… But she supposed she'd just have to wait and see.

The wind gushed into her window refreshingly. She breathed it in, her smile lingering. This place wasn't at all what she used to expect.

I could definitely get used to this, she thought contently. Hangman's Tree could really be her home if she truly wished. This room could be hers. These boys could be her family.

She couldn't help but dwell on the fantasy. No more lying. No more holding back. The Lost Boys would understand, of course. That she was sure of.

Jane could have it all.

She could stay there, forever.

It all relied on one simple choice.

Her eyes fell on Pan—no, better get used to calling him Peter. He sat on a stump in the corner of the hideout, watching the game before him. The sun shone on his auburn locks, dusting it with gold.

Jane huffed her bangs out of her eyes—a new addition since she'd arrived—trying to keep all that silly nonsense out of her head.

Quit your ogling, she scolded herself.

Before she could change her mind, she took hold of the rope outside her window and lowered herself down. Her heart pounded in her chest.

● ● ●

I can't believe I'm doing this.

When she rounded the tree, she froze. Her stomach dropped. Hastily, she backed away before they could see her. Jane took a breath, peaked behind the tree, and took in the scene.

Tootles stood near Peter like a shadow, silently flinging stones at the ground with his slingshot. Peter wasn't smiling. Forlornly, he held something to his mouth, elbow on his knee as he supported his chin. His brown eyes were ghostly, unrecognizable. Jane zeroed in on what it was he held to his lips, something strung around his neck with a leather string.

Jane's throat tightened.

It was a silver thimble and a bronze acorn.

She instantly knew what they were thinking about, *who* they were thinking about. And it dawned on her yet again why she couldn't stay forever. She'd already made her choice. The only problem was that now she was not so sure it was the right one.

*****

"There you are," Hazel chimed, fluttering up to her. "You look so much better!"

Alice smiled at the fairy. She certainly felt better, clean and refreshed. Her stomach was full, her clothes were new, and she could've slept for days for all she cared. When she'd woken from her nap, she found her hair had been braided with blue flowers while she was asleep. Hopefully the fairies didn't go much farther than that.

The grass felt soft under her, and her feet enjoyed the cool of the pond. Hazel flew over and sat on Alice's knee, which was a strange experience but not one she couldn't get used to. She felt the urge to ask something, but just as quickly she forgot it. Alice hoped it wasn't anything important.

"We hardly ever receive guests, especially new ones," Hazel rambled. "Tiger Lily never comes anymore and Peter doesn't visit like he used to. A few Lost Boys stop by occasionally, but not very often. I suppose you don't know who I'm talking about."

"You'd be surprised," Alice admitted, still vaguely bothered at forgetting her question. "Why don't they come anymore?"

"Well, for one, they're boys," Hazel huffed, tossing her braid over her shoulder. "Most would prefer to go hunting or fighting rather than hang out with us when most of them can't even understand the way we speak. They don't really bother asking if we might want to join them."

"Would you?"

"I don't know; they haven't invited me! But anyway, besides that, they have to try harder to survive and defend their hideout now. It's gotten so big that it's hardly a *hideout* anymore. Even the Island can't hide something so large for very long."

"Why don't you just go and visit Hangman's Tree?"

Hazel rubbed her little hand over her gold armband sheepishly. "Most fairies prefer to stay in Pixie Hollow. It's home. Also, it's not always easy to be a fairy in Neverland where predators lurk around every corner and rain falls without warning."

Alice smirked. "I can attest to that."

"You were pretty soaked when you came in."

A group of fairies flew by, smiling shyly at Alice and a few giving Hazel a friendly wave. But they didn't stay. Hazel rubbed her hands down her braid self-consciously, doe eyes following the group until they disappeared behind a glittering tree.

Alice paused a moment before questioning, "*Most* fairies prefer to stay in Pixie Hollow?"

Hazel blushed slightly. "Well, Tinker Bell doesn't stay all the time. She has her own nook over at Hangman's Tree. She's been Peter's first mate since as long as either of them can remember. Tink was always the outgoing type, the only fairy who knows this island by heart. But Tink would always come home eventually."

"So, you two are close, huh?"

Hazel nodded. "Tink's my best friend. She used to take me to Hangman's Tree for visits sometimes. We'd go explore the Island. But, I decided to stay here when she said she was going to search for her friend. As outgoing as I am, I don't think I could handle leaving Neverland."

Alice started to open her mouth to ask another question when a searing pain hit the top of her head. Her ears rang. She cried out involuntarily. Hazel jumped back in surprise, her wings coming to her aid as she hovered in midair. The pain lingered, but the shock of it subsided. Alice rubbed her aching head.

"*Borogove!*" she hissed.

Hazel's eyes were wide; she flew around Alice's head like a dragonfly. "I thought I sensed a curse! Are you cursed?"

Alice shook her head and groaned. "I'm just paying a price. It was a sacrifice I was willing to make."

• • •

Hazel studied her for a moment, hovering just above Alice's knee.

Alice wondered what the Mad Hatter had done back in Wonderland. He probably bumped his head on the bottom of a table when retrieving a needle or pen. Or maybe one of the Brothers Tweedle gave him a knock on the head. Perhaps the Cheshire Cat dropped a pot or a glass flower on him unexpectedly. Either way, Alice tried not to think of what could happen if an incident like that happened again, but in a far more dangerous situation.

She furrowed her brow. Did she ever tell Remus about the new ties between them? She couldn't remember. But even so, she supposed he would realize soon enough. Either she would get hurt and he'd feel it, so Celeste would've told him. Still, it was odd how she couldn't even recall whether or not she'd told him.

Borogove, what was that question...?

With a silent flutter of wings, Hazel sat back down on Alice's knee, doe eyes examining her as if reading her mind.

Hazel sighed, shook her head in either pity or sympathy—Alice couldn't tell. "I couldn't imagine making such a sacrifice, even for love."

Alice wondered if the pixie really could read her mind. "I guess people do truly mad things for those they love."

"Yes, I suppose they do," Hazel admitted, though she still seemed skeptical.

In rapid speed, a fairy flew up to them and jostled to a halt. It was the first male fairy Alice had seen up close. His brown skin was splattered in dirt and pixie dust, acorn hat askew over a mane of chocolate curls. Mud streaked his face and glitter clung to his eyebrows as if he'd face planted into a flowerbed.

When he spoke, the bells in his voice were deep like bronze. "I managed to contact Tink." He flew right up to Hazel when his face twisted to confusion as if he caught an unusual odor. "Do I smell a curse?"

"Sort of," Alice and Hazel said simultaneously.

"What'd she say?" Hazel pressed anxiously.

"Well, it's not much, but apparently she's still on the Mainland. She'll be here as soon as she can, probably by tomorrow."

Alice frowned. "I thought you couldn't contact her?"

"No, we can, thanks to Sparrow." Hazel grinned. "He discovered how pixie dust can be used to send messages to other fairies. You know, in case of an emergency."

Sparrow's face grew red. He twiddled his hands as if they longed for something to do.

Hazel turned doe eyes back on Sparrow hopefully. "Has Tink found her yet?"

Sparrow shook his head sadly. "No. Even Tink is starting to lose hope. I think she's beginning to believe what everyone else seems to know."

She sighed. "Poor Tink. I bet it's hard for her, finding out her friend's dead."

Something clicked, but it was like grasping at water that kept slipping from her hands. Still grasping, Alice voiced, "Who is Tink's friend that everyone keeps talking about?"

"She's a human girl who used to live with the Lost Boys until the pirates captured and killed her," Hazel said softly. "Her name was—"

"Wendy."

CHAPTER EIGHT
TIGER LILY

The Panther Tribe's camp was exactly as Wendy remembered. Teepees and wigwams stood side by side with a few longhouses and even platform dwellings. A single totem pole stood high above all in the camp's center, a symbol of every ancestral tribe they knew of represented on the structure.

The camp buzzed with life. A group of women sat in a circle weaving, sewing, laughing, chatting. Children ran around in different forms of play, snatching unobserved food, chasing overexcited dogs, decorating sleeping old men in feathers and beads. Some men and women were carving things out of wood and bone in one corner. Young and old played music on pipes and drums in another. All in all, there was none who weren't busy in some form or fashion—except for perhaps the few old men getting a makeover while they slept.

The group of hunters around Wendy and Red dispersed into the camp with their kills to awaiting families and friends. Only the tribesmen who first captured the girls stayed with them.

Wendy felt her stomach clench. How could she get out of this predicament? She was sure she could somehow use this to her advantage if she were only clever enough. But trying to get Tiger Lily to do something... It would all be pointless lest she could find a way to make the Tribe's Princess believe she could get something out of it.

Just think! How can I get Tiger Lily to release us willingly without her killing me?

. . .

The prospect still felt exceedingly impossible by the time Wendy and Red were led into a large teepee. The only thing that gave her a smidge of hope was perhaps if she only spoke to the Chief, he would be more reasonable.

The two were indicated to take a seat on the floor, which they did so without complaint. Wendy watched as their captors split up, some staying guard, others off to find Tiger Lily no doubt.

"Wendy," Red whispered, drawing her from her thoughts. "There are children here."

Wendy looked at her friend curiously. "Yes?"

"But I thought that the only children in Neverland were, you know, the Lost Boys."

Wendy could not help but smile, shaking her head. "No, there are other children in Neverland besides the Lost Boys. The Tribe, the pirates, they have children though not nearly so many."

"But no one in Neverland grows up?"

"If they didn't, there'd be a very short amount of tribesmen and pirates, now wouldn't there? With all the fighting, feuds, dangers and all."

Wendy's mind was still racing, but she tried to answer Red's questions as best she could. It was a strain, but she'd learned long ago to juggle different trains of thought at once. It saved time.

"Does that mean the only ones who can't grow up are Peter and the Lost Boys?"

"No." Wendy shook her head. "No one in Neverland can grow up."

"Then how do they?"

● ● ●

Wendy sighed. "You know how Lost Boys come to Neverland?"

Red nodded. "They come in on boats from our world."

"Yes, and that's how they keep up their numbers," Wendy continued. "But it's different for everyone else. The fairies are born from any child's first laugh. The beasts slink in through portals from other worlds. Kyta was created from imagination, just as Neverland was, which is why she cannot be killed; she lives off the greatest ideas and wonders in all the worlds. From where the mermaids come from is debatable. They could be products of nightmares, or criminals sent to the lagoon as prisoners, or the survivors of those who supposedly died at sea."

A scuffle outside grabbed her attention. But after a moment, it proved nothing to be concerned about.

"The pirates and tribesmen maintain existence the same way," Wendy went on. "They raise their children. The pirates will typically go out to sea just to the boundaries of Neverland where its powers of youth tend to be weakest. That's where they raise their children, though it takes them a lot longer to grow older. As for the Panther Tribe, I suppose you could say they migrate."

Red furrowed her eyebrows. "Migrate?"

"They leave Neverland during the cold weather," she explained. "I'm not sure where they go, maybe the Mainland. But when the time comes, the Tribe pack up their belongings and ride their canoes beyond Neverland's boundaries. They always return in the spring. But the tribesmen age half as fast, though much faster than the pirates."

● ● ●

"So, that's all you have to do to leave Neverland?" Red asked. "You just sail away?"

"In the long run, yes, but you never know where you'll end up," Wendy answered, mind still racing, "unless you can fly."

Commotion sounded outside the tent, jerking them from conversation. The scramble of feet mixed with urgent voices in the Panther Tribe's language. Wendy watched the tent flap expectantly, back straighter, head higher. She half expected a knife to come out for her.

The flap flew back and a small group of tribesmen entered. Wendy's stomach tightened, neck stiff.

Tiger Lily's amber flecked eyes glared right into hers. Wendy suppressed the urge to shift. Tension shifted through the air.

Tiger Lily barked an order, ripping through the silence. Wendy didn't catch it, as it was in her own tongue, but its meaning was clear as soon as the other tribesmen left. The teepee seemed stifling.

She hadn't changed much since last Wendy saw her, though the headdress was new. Tiger Lily had always been taller than her, but only for the past decade and a half had she appeared older than her. Beneath the headdress, her onyx hair was braided with feathers. Every feature seemed hard and soft in a way that made her look dangerous, frightening, and beautiful all at once.

The tent flap was pushed back yet again and Red gave an unintentional start, though Wendy didn't flinch. A sleek black panther slinked inside to stand beside Tiger Lily. His yellow eyes watched Red intently, whiskers twitching ever so slightly.

Finally, Tiger Lily spoke, "So, you are back from the dead, I see."

Wendy swallowed through the knot in her throat, the only sign of confusion she permitted to show. *Back from the dead?* What did that mean?

"Seems I am," Wendy responded anyway, concealing all hesitation. "Hello Tiger Lily; Bagheera."

The panther's yellow eyes flicked to her. She extended her hand for Bagheera to sniff. After affirming her identity, Bagheera gave an affectionate chuff. He circled back to his mistress, placing himself beside her as she sat cross legged on the floor. She'd always thought it funny that Tiger Lily had named her panther after a character from one of the stories she used to relay to the Lost Boys.

"What are you doing here?" Tiger Lily questioned.

"Your warriors didn't give us much choice in the matter," Wendy responded, allowing some edge in her tone. "Believe me, if it was up to us, we'd be at Hangman's Tree by now."

"*We?*"

Amber flecked eyes switched to Red as if only just realizing she was there. Wendy watched Red meet Tiger Lily's gaze with the same cool ferocity.

The Panther Tribe's Princess turned back to Wendy. "Where did you find this cursed one?"

She noticed Red's jaw clench, fingers curling to a fist. Wendy didn't blame her for getting angry over such an accusation. Unfortunately, now wasn't the time or the place. She placed her hand over Red's and gave it a reassuring squeeze.

* * *

"Red is a close friend; we've been through a lot together," Wendy regarded. "I trust her with my life."

Red glanced at her appreciatively, relaxing some. Good. They couldn't afford a brawl at the moment. Tiger Lily merely grunted, eyes examining Red again grimly. She didn't move a muscle as her gaze returned to Wendy, an action that made her want to squirm.

"You have not been to see the Lost Boys?" Tiger Lily inquired.

"No," Wendy answered, deciding to conceal the whole truth by speaking truth. "We haven't had the chance. We only just arrived the other day."

"How? The Island did not tell of your arrival."

Wendy hesitated, her throat feeling dry. She didn't want to mention the White Rabbit's pocket watch; that kind of information couldn't be shared lightly. If word got out about their quest to find this ultimate Master, who knew what could happen. It probably wouldn't be good. And Wendy didn't trust Tiger Lily who could just as predictably save a life as she could take one.

"A portal," Wendy quickly decided, which wasn't far from the truth. "We stumbled upon a portal that some of the beasts come through. The Island doesn't tremble at the use of such portals."

Tiger Lily grunted again. Her gaze steady, she seemed to be calculating a plan or theory. Typical of her. Always trying to find the advantage of a situation for her own gain. She was probably wondering if there was something better to do with Wendy than kill her, weighing her options. Wendy met Tiger Lily's assessing stare coolly,

• • •

wondering herself how to turn this situation for her advantage.

If only she could act more like Peter would. He'd start to smile, most likely, and pull as much smooth talk as he could in his cocky, likeable kind of way. He would demand such a position that he'd seem to be the authority in any situation. Wendy had seen him do it before many times. He could make tribesmen forget who was the real Chief, make pirates feel as if they were the prisoners, even sometimes work such charm on the mermaids that they lost the desire to drag him to the lagoon's depths.

But Peter wasn't here now. And Wendy wasn't sure she could pull off such cocky and charming confidence.

Finally, she broke the silence, trying to hide the tone of exasperation, "Will you let us go?"

Tiger Lily never changed expression. "Why should I? We have never been friends. My tribe has formed no temporary allegiance with the Lost Boys."

"But what if you did?" she inquired urgently.

Tiger Lily actually looked shocked. Even Red seemed surprised at the prospect. Of course, the Lost Boys and the Panther Tribe had formed allegiances before, but it was always Peter Pan who proposed such things, never the other way around.

Now I have your attention, Wendy thought. *It's time to seal the deal.*

"What if we did form an allegiance?" Wendy repeated, trying not to lose momentum. "Together, we could rise up against our common enemy: the pirates. Just let me talk with the Chief. I know he'd like hear the benefits of it."

Tiger Lily's back snapped straighter and her expression became dangerously grave. "You have indeed been gone a long time. My father has long since died, killed by the Hook's own blade. I am High Chieftess now."

Wendy's heart fell. The Chief was dead? She couldn't believe it. It wasn't like they were ever close; many times they were on opposing sides. But he'd always been... there; a presence in Neverland that she never thought would be missing. Now the Chief of the Panther Tribe was dead.

Wendy dropped her gaze. "I'm so sorry, Tiger Lily."

Tiger Lily's face remained stony, but her eyes betrayed the war between strength and sorrow. She'd never noticed before how very old her eyes were until then. Wendy wondered if her own eyes revealed such age.

"So," Red thankfully interrupted the heavy silence, "about this allegiance?"

Wendy thought she almost saw gratitude in those amber speckled eyes. "If we are to join forces then it must be further discussed. I will talk to my warriors and elders until I reach a decision."

All three of them rose, the panther also standing. Tiger Lily locked eyes with Red with a brief nod, as much of an apology as she would ever give. Then she turned to Wendy, and again she wondered if Tiger Lily would change her mind and kill her on the spot. But though there was no trust between them, there was a sense of mutual respect. Wendy knew they would never be friends—the ridge between them was far too wide—but at least that respect was there. Maybe that alone was the thing that stayed their urge to kill each other.

• • •
65

Without another word, Tiger Lily whipped around and left the tent. Bagheera quickly rubbed against Wendy's legs and circled Red twice before following his mistress. The flap swished shut, leaving Wendy and Red alone in the teepee.

Wendy let out a breath she didn't know she'd been holding. Relief flooded through her. "We did it."

"What exactly did we do?" Red asked. "What does this mean?"

There were so many things Wendy could've responded with. With the pending attack on the pirates, that would mean they could potentially find more information about the Master at Blind Man's Bluff. If they attack, they could even flush out the Master himself, especially if Hook proves to be the one. But that wasn't why she was so happy.

Wendy grinned. "We'll finally go to Hangman's Tree."

*****

A rapid knocking sounded on the door of the Captain's Quarters.

"You may come in," Hook permitted without looking up.

Mister Smee came bustling inside. He removed his red sock of a hat when he entered the cabin, exposing a large bald spot on top of his head. Mister Smee was a short, round man, who could just as easily be mistaken for a professor as he would a pirate. Half-moon spectacles perched on the bridge of his round nose. A strip of white hair went around the back of his head and fed into short sideburns. The only distinctively dangerous thing about him was the strangely twisted sword strapped to his hip, and the flintlock pistols holstered across his torso.

"Good afternoon, Captain," Mister Smee greeted cheerily.

"Hello, Mister Smee." Hook smiled the only grin he had, though it was still frightening.

"Fine day today, isn't it, Captain?" He stated, tottering around the cabin for things to do: hang discarded clothes, straighten the décor, down the last remnants of brandy in abandoned goblets. All the while he seemed to rock back and forth on his feet.

"Yes, it is a fine day, I suppose," Hook agreed. "And how would you be, Mister Smee?"

"Fine and dandy, Captain," Mister Smee assured, beating off the dust in the curtains.

"Ole Johnny Corkscrew holding up?"

Mister Smee patted the hilt of his sword. "Yep! Ole Johnny's holding up real fine."

"That's good to hear," Hook said, turning the page of his ledger with his hook. "Anything to report?"

"Nothing really, Captain. The ship is sailing smooth and fine. We should be approaching Peg Leg Point this time tomorrow."

"Excellent," Hook said, waiting expectedly with a raised eyebrow.

Mister Smee always had something more to say than just the typical small talk. Being a man who enjoyed gossip, he always knew what was going on around him whether true or false. Rumors were what made him go round. If there was anything Mister Smee loved more than knowing that latest gossip, it was telling Hook about it. And Hook had a knack for finding the truth in such rumors one way or another.

"You know, Captain," Smee began, "I'll stand by you 'til me last breath. You are my Captain, after all. Been my best pal since we were wee lads, you have."

"Yes, Mister Smee."

"And you know how much I agree with your big plan. It's a brilliant one, after all. Never was there a better pirate than you. Your plan's the finest I've heard yet."

Always the flatterer, Mister Smee was. It was one of the many things Hook liked about the man.

"Now, as for the crew, they seem to think a different story."

Hook's blue eyes darted up, smile tightening devilishly. "And what are they thinking, Mister Smee?"

"Well, Captain, some of the crew's a bit fidgety about what's or who's the big bloke behind the operation. They say that you be fiddling with dark magic, things that'd best not be fiddled with. Now, this is them speaking, not me. I stand by you, just as I said. But the crew's getting uneasy, them not knowing who's it we're working for and all. As for me, I'm all for the whole mystery boss, as long as you are. They're starting to say you don't know what it is you're doing or getting into. This is the crew, not me. I know you know what you're doing. But the crew's still a little fidgety."

"So," Hook growled threateningly, "the crew's getting cold feet, eh?"

"The crew is, not me, of course," Mister Smee corrected.

"Of course," Hook's voice was sickly smooth, eyes calculating. "I'm thinking I need to speak to my crew."

• • •

68

Captain Hook stood dangerously, taking heavy steps to the door. Mister Smee hastened to open them for him before he could reach them, almost tripping over his own feet. Hook stomped purposefully out on deck where the crew was working, climbing the steps to the quarterdeck where he stood in view of everyone on the ship. All froze where they were; every eye turned to their Captain.

Hook glowered down at them. "As I understand it, some of you don't agree with the plan I have to seek revenge on that blasted Pan and his little brats. What was it you'd said they were thinking, Mister Smee?"

"That you don't know what you're doing," Smee answered, somehow ending up by his side.

"*That I don't know what I'm doing*," Hook annunciated every word as if every syllable were being picked off by his claw.

All were silent as he slowly descended the steps again to the main deck. His iron hook scrapped the railing eerily, bone chilling. As soon as he stepped on the deck, he approached the table where a group pirates had been playing hazard. All players looked up at him, trying not to shake in their boots.

Captain Hook cracked a laugh, smile stretching across his face. The crew looked at each other uncertainly, but as their Captain seemed to shrug off the incident, they began to laugh uneasily, slowly growing more comfortable. No one seemed to notice how Hook's smile never reached his eyes. They did notice when he suddenly tossed the gaming table in enraged fury. Dice, cards, and doubloons went flying every which way. The table hurtled into the unsuspecting game players.

• • •

"YOU THINK I DON'T KNOW WHAT I'M DOING?!" Hook bellowed, spit flying from his mouth as he trumped around the deck in a rampage. "YOU THINK I DON'T KNOW WHAT I'VE AGREED TOO?!"

The crew hastened to shake their heads frantically. The Captain waved his iron claw dangerously about, nearly hitting most everyone within range. One unlucky bloke ended up with his cheek ripped open in a single blow.

"You scurvy dogs don't know who you're dealing with!" He exclaimed in a passion, "You want to question me? Question my decisions? Then you tell me to my face! But what I'm hearing is *mutiny!* I'LL SEND YOU ALL DOWN TO DAVY JONES' LOCKER IF I HAVE TO!"

Hook drew his cutlass, forcing those around him to back away. He was dangerous when he got into a temper. There was no telling what he would do.

"You're worried about *black magic?* You're worried about we we're working with?" He cried, "I DON'T CARE IF I HAVE TO WORK WITH THE DEVIL HIMSELF IF IT MEANS BEING RID OF THAT *BLASTED* PAN AND HIS BAND OF *BLOODY* LOST BOYS!"

The crew quickly began stammering apologies, whether or not they had anything to be sorry for. There were few things that could bring a pirate to his knees. Captain James Hook was one of them.

Breathing heavily, Hook lowered his cutlass and began to regain his composure. "Does anyone have anything to say?"

"No, Captain," everyone chanted at once.

"Then get back to work."

*****

• • •

Wendy and Red sat around the only campfire that would accept them without harsh or suspenseful stares. The children, on the other hand, only looked at them in curiosity and even mischief. Already they'd managed to try and trick them into eating insects. Red wasn't fooled, and neither was Wendy, though she popped the bugs in her mouth despite it. That earned her a stream of giggles.

"You know what that was, right?" Red asked her.

Wendy shrugged, not bothering to explain how often the Lost Boys had *accidentally* fed her even nastier things than insects. Even so, it took a while to get the legs out of her teeth.

An elder woman wearing a colorful shawl around her and carrying long strings of beads came over, village dogs at her heals. She sat on the opposite side of the fire where the children hurriedly plopped on the floor as near as they dared, bright eyes wide in expectation. Wendy watched as the woman's knotted, papery hands wrestled and stroked her beads. In her own language, the elder spoke in recognizable rhythm, like a spell, like a story.

The dogs trotted over and made a beeline for Red, sniffing her face and licking her hands. She sighed in slight annoyance. But two dogs settled to lay their heads on her lap, whilst two more curled up to rest at her back. Wendy smiled slightly. Red shrugged in defeat.

"What's she saying?" she asked, caving in and scratching the dogs behind the ears.

"Stories," Wendy said easily, listening to the flow of the woman's words. "Probably the one about the Neverbird, how it led the Tribe to Neverland. That's a popular one."

But she really couldn't be sure. She knew some of the Panther Tribe's language, but not much. The captivation on the children's face, the way some held their breath or mouths hung open, perhaps it wasn't the story of the Neverbird after all.

The fire flicked, reaching for the stars. The moons shone brightly down on them, making the sea glow silver. Crashing, sloshing, Wendy could imagine the waves throwing themselves against the cliff's face. A melancholy serenity lay over her as she felt it all, the words, the moons, the waves. Night was alive, perhaps even more than the day.

Her ears pricked at something the elder woman spoke, a single word she did know that sounded like a sad and passionate crow.

Pan.

She hadn't even realized she'd said it aloud.

The elder woman looked up at her with black eyes. "You know the song?"

Wendy nodded grimly. There was only one story the woman could mean, the one she called *song*. But it wasn't a tune, just verses meant to be spoken in reverence to the events they recounted. Drums or flute could be added, panpipe being the most popular, but the words… they were too heavy to carry melody.

The woman looked at her expectantly, chin dipping as if in a bow. Wendy sighed, watching the flames, only able to imagine Peter's face when the story was told before him. It wasn't just a story to him. He'd lived it.

When Wendy spoke the verses, the elder woman echoed her in the Tribe's tongue:

"Just a boy, Just a child,
In a place where no one grows up;
Young bodies with old minds,
Dream and nightmare reign side by side,
In a place where no one grows up;
A time when darkness shrouded the sun,
Vengeance birthed from sea and blood,
Many had fallen in the war never won,
In a place where no one grows up;
When the boy's heart grieved he became more of a man,
When the pirate's heart hardened with the loss of his hand,
One dreadful night everything changed and feuds began,
Now the ghosts from their mistakes are tied to this land,
In a place where no one grows up;
Just a boy, just a child, in appearance it's true,
But children can carry terrible burdens too,
For sometimes stopping time doesn't mean forever youth,
Living, forgetting, loving, seething, bearing an all too heavy
truth;
Just a boy, Just a child,
In a place where no one grows up."

Wendy listened as the elder woman finished the final line in dutiful echo, dutiful melancholy. She'd heard from Peter what happened on the day the feud started. She was aware of the details, about the bloody battle between Lost Boy and pirate, the transformation of both Pan and Hook. But as terrible as the scenes in her mind could imagine it, there was never a more pained expression than Peter's when he remembered it. It was a memory even Neverland couldn't dull or take away.

• • •

Stories help us remember, Wendy thought to herself, *what we never want to forget.*

Red tapped her arm, bringing her attention back to the present.

Whispers rippled over the group of children. Wendy turned to see Tiger Lily standing behind her, the amber in her eyes dancing in the firelight.

The Chieftess stood fixedly, as if tasting the words in her mouth before releasing them. "We leave at dawn."

CHAPTER NINE

THE LAGOON

Kai burst through the thicket and came to an abrupt halt as his feet skidded over stones. A great lagoon stretched out before him, bordered by a pebble beach, its surface a perfectly reflective mirror. Hardly a ripple disturbed the reflection of sky and forestry on its three sides. At the lagoon's back was the ocean, reaching out past the horizon in cerulean waves. There was a point where the lagoon met the sea, where silvery reflective waters ended and tropical blue began. Two bodies of water that met but never mixed. The only thing penetrating the lagoon's smooth surface was a single rock that sat in its center: Marooner's Rock.

Anger and frustration built up inside Kai's chest. The pirate had lied. This obviously wasn't Hangman's Tree. And he wasn't in the least bit surprised either, which made him even more angry. He never should have trusted that devilish brute.

Kai kicked at the ground in frustration, sending up a shower of pebbled. Irritated, he raked his fingers through his disheveled hair. What was he supposed to do now? He couldn't go aimlessly around the island; that wasn't always the best way to find what you're looking for. Unless he found a Lost Boy, he couldn't just ask for directions for the chance of being deceived again.

Kai racked his brain for anything that could help him. But on a mind that hadn't obtained any sleep last night, he wasn't getting anywhere.

Scratching his jaw, the itchy stubble annoyed him more than usual. Turning to take in his surroundings once more, maybe find an idea over his shoulder, his gaze landed in the rocky shores of the lagoon. His heart leapt to his throat, stomach tightening, and he suddenly felt as if his legs would fail him.

"Gerda," Kai breathed with such pain and longing no lament could ever match it.

She was exactly as he remembered, back when they were happy, when they were together. Bare feet soaking in the cool lagoon waters, Gerda sat on the rocky shore, pink skirt swept over her knees, golden hair hanging loosely over the dress' sandy bodice. Wildflowers were braided around her head like a crown. She stared over the lagoon, sunbeams kissing her freckles.

Kai's feet took over. He ran toward her, heart pounding loudly in his ears. As if she sensed him approaching, Gerda turned her beautiful face toward him, soft features naturally taking on a warm smile.

"Kai," she sighed, hastening to her feet.

It took only a moment more for Kai to reach her. Enfolding her in his tight embrace, he held her as if she would melt at any moment, held her as if his entire being couldn't hold together if she disappeared. His hands trembled. *She's real; she's here.* Tears welling up in his eyes and his throat clenched in a hard knot as he absorbed her presence. He felt Gerda's warm breath on his chest, the way her arms clung around his waist in her own self-assurance.

"I thought I lost you," Kai whispered in her hair.

"You'll never lose me," Gerda reassured.

He pulled back, holding her face in his hands. "But, how…?"

• • •

She put her hands over his, so delicate yet roughened. "It doesn't matter how. What matters is that I'm here, right now, with you."

Before he could even think about pursuing the question, Gerda pressed her lips to his and the world fell away.

So many old memories, happy memories he hadn't thought of in ages, filled his mind with all the bliss as if he lived them again. It was so real. When Gerda began to pull away, the memories clouded over, fading. Desperate, he drew closer, pushing away all the pain and the sorrows reality would bring, accepting the euphoria of reliving the past when life was simpler, when life was good.

But then the wrong memory came up.

He remembered everything.

They walked hand in hand into a place of their own discovery; they'd called it their *smultronställe*. Fresh mountain air swept into the meadow, pleasantly cool. A garland of wildflowers sat on Gerda's golden hair, a thick braid wrapped around her head like a crown. She held her boots in one hand for she simply refused to go around on such a beautiful day with them on. Her face was bright; she didn't even need a smile for it to show. She was so beautiful.

Kai remembered how nervous he had been, hands sweaty, face hot. But he'd been determined despite his nerves. Before he realized it, he was gripping her shoulders tenderly, their faces only breaths apart. Gerda seemed shocked. He almost lost his nerve. He remembered the way her lips curved ever so slightly, the way her eyes twinkled before she kissed him for the first time.

The memory vanished as Kai pulled away, realization hitting him hard. He felt dizzy.

"What is it?" Gerda asked, concerned.

"This is wrong," Kai mumbled, shaking his fuzzy head. "This is all wrong. It can't be real. *You* can't be real."

"What are you talking about? Of course I'm real! I'm right here, Kai."

She caught his eye, but that only made his blood run cold. Silvery pools reflecting the lagoon's surface perfectly stared right through his very soul. Those eyes, he didn't know them.

"You're not Gerda," Kai growled, anger leaking through his confusion. "You're a… a sorceress!"

She smiled, all previous countenance melting away. A lump formed in his throat, hating how much she really did look like Gerda despite the foreign expression and ghostly eyes. He almost lost his balance, then he realized where he stood.

"You flatter me," the illusion of Gerda crooned, voice changing to a silky tone like the sea washing against the shore, "but a sorceress I am not."

The water broke under his feet and Kai sank like a rock straight into the lagoon. He held his breath, straining to keep from losing it all at once. Underwater, it was clearer than should've been possible. Hands grasped his arms, pushing him deeper. The mermaid still had Gerda's face, but her body changed to the creature she truly was, powerful tail, scaly forearms.

A swarm of mermaids emerged from the lagoon's depths through a stream of bubbles. Skeletons of past victims littered the floor far beneath them. Kai snapped out of his

• • •

shock, struggling against the mermaid's strong hold. It only slowed their decent. Grasping for every ounce of strength within him, he kicked her right in the stomach. He tried to ignore Gerda's face as it twisted in pain as he stuck out again. She recoiled. Kai struggled to swim up and away.

His head broke the surface, air filling his burning lungs. Looking around for attackers, he couldn't see anything beneath the cursed mirror waters. The shore was too far away, he evaluated. He'd never make it. Marooner's Rock was closer. If he got there, maybe he could buy some time...

Something grabbed his ankle. Kai had a split second to hold his breath before he was dragged under. Mermaids surrounded him instantly, wrestling each other to drown him. This time, his head was clear enough for instincts to kick in.

Instantly, Kai had his stolen knife in hand and slashed through the water, bubbles exploding, blade ripping through skin. A sheer scream echoed around them. Crimson blood clouded the clear water. The mermaids retreated instinctively save for one.

The illusion of Gerda's dead face was the last thing Kai saw before breaking the surface again.

Taking in deep gulps of air, Kai swam as hard as he could toward Marooner's Rock. Water splashed around him as mermaids came after him with a new thirst for vengeance. An arm jutted out for him and all he saw was sharp teeth and reflective eyes as he jammed his knife into her collarbone. He kept on in rapid strokes, limbs on fire.

He was just over a meter away from reaching the boulder when a sharp blow launched into his ribs and clamped on, sinking into his flesh. He cried out, locked his breath, and was thrown over. Searing pain burst through his side as the mermaid locked down in a secure bite, sending them both rolling through the water. Kai didn't know how many times they broke the surface before he bashed his fist against her face and forced her to release him. Saltwater stung his wound, bleeding freely now. Kai rushed to the surface, losing energy but bursting with adrenaline. When the mermaid came after him again, he swam harder, avoiding her teeth.

Reaching Marooner's Rock at last, Kai clambered up its rough side. The mermaid following him just managed to trip him, his legs slipping on the wet slime and hitting his chin hard on the rock. Before she could try another attempt, he managed to scramble to his feet and reach the top.

Panting hard, not bothering to wipe the blood off of his chin, he looked around him. Scarlet ribbons rippled through the mirror lagoon waters. He felt so heavy. The bite wound on his side screamed in pain. Showers of saltwater sprayed up as mermaids broke the surface all around, barnacled hands groping for him. He held his knife out threateningly, pushing aside exhaustion. It didn't take long for them to try and climb the rock. He stamped on hands that clawed up toward him, kicking the mermaids who managed to get up farther. It only made them angrier.

Kai caught the eye of a familiar brown skinned mermaid glaring at him with such hatred and determination. He could see it coming right before it happened. She launched into the air, over her struggling sistren, and snatched his right foot in a death grip. The barnacles on her hands dug into his skin through his boot. Before he could even think how to react, the mermaid yanked his foot out from under him just as something latched onto both of his shoulders and pulled Kai into the air. The mermaids screamed in frustration.

He was too stunned to shout out a proper curse.

Right as he noticed the brown skinned mermaid still hadn't released his foot during his elevation, a sickening snap resonated in his ears and an explosion of pain shot up his ankle. His ears rang. The mermaid still didn't let go, dragged through the water and splashing water everywhere. Neither did the thing carrying him drop him in its continuous flight.

Pain still raged, drowning out most confusion and shock. Gritting his teeth; in one swift and rash movement, Kai smashed his free leg down on the mermaid's arms, freeing him from her barnacled grasp and jolting his ankle painfully. He couldn't feel or move his foot.

As the mermaids' angry screams raged on in the ever increasing distance, relief blossomed inside his chest. His ankle throbbed, and his side burned like fire. His relief ebbed away as he took in his present situation. Despite his attempts, Kai couldn't see what still carried him into the air, nor could he see where it was taking him.

One thing was clear: It wasn't taking him back to the Island.

*****

Finally, Jane was able to join one of their adventures. She was so elated it never occurred to her what kind of venture they might partake, what they would do, what they might find. Cutlass strapped to her side, face streaked with mud, she proudly walked with the other boys following Pan through the jungle.

She recognized Slightly, who held his short bow over his shoulder and had his fox mask pushed up over his matted orange hair, and Curly also, his big brawn figure hard to miss or disguise even with a bear mask covering his dark face. She didn't recognize the other two, one with black hair and a small nose, the other with onyx skin and the mask of a warthog. Neither one looked over ten.

The jungle was loud, but unusually bright as light filtered through the leaves. Jane wondered where they were going, or if Peter was leaving it to the Island to decide. Though she knew that maps of Neverland assumed general locations of key places, the Island itself could prove unpredictable in where you'll end up or what it concealed.

Her point seemed to be made clear around the next turn. A river ran below them in a series of pools and small waterfalls, the water so clear she could see right to the bottom. The ledge where they stood was a good seven meters above a broad pool with a rushing waterfall to the right. It was beautiful, even though the mosquitoes were abundant where they stood.

Peter looked back at her, eyes glittering in a way that made her stomach twist in knots. With a crow, he turned and launched himself off the ledge, doing a backflip for good measure before he landed with a splash in the water. Jane looked down, worried the water wasn't deep enough for such a dive. But Peter popped back up laughing, swimming joyously.

Slightly came running past her, mask and weapons thrown off before he went over, his dive less graceful but just as exuberant as Peter's. Jane couldn't help but laugh when Slightly emerged sputtering and splashing while he gained buoyancy. The two other Lost Boys came in splashing on either side of him.

● ● ●

"Come on, Jane!" Peter shouted encouragingly.

Slightly sprayed water from his mouth like a fountain, then added, "The water's great! No piranhas or anything!"

"What's a piranha?" the small nosed boy questioned, his pale face glowing from the water's reflection.

"No idea."

Jane turned to Curly, who removed his mask and set it beside his heavy club on the ground. He smiled shyly, but of course that playful boyishness lay behind it.

"Right behind you," he assured.

Such the gentleman, she thought to herself, removing her boots and cutlass.

Looking over the edge again, she felt a surge of adrenaline. She backed up, took a breath, and gave a running start before leaping off the ledge. Arms flailing, she held her breath right before she crashed into the pool. Water rushed up her nose. A moment of cold daggers hit her all at once before she adapted to the temperature and broke the surface, sputtering, coughing, and laughing all at once.

She barely had time to wipe the hair out of her eyes before there was a shout and a crash, water spraying everywhere as Curly cannonballed into the pool. Tossed underwater again, her vision was drowned with bubbles. She came up spraying water like Slightly had, laughing openly with the others as Curly emerged in a burst.

The mud quickly washed off her face as they swam and splashed and dunked each other underwater. Such happiness Jane couldn't remember ever knowing. Overcome with such bliss, she floated down the pool with eyes closed, letting the sun's warmth wash over her face. She half expected someone to flip her over, but she didn't care. The

Lost Boys were too busy trying to dunk Curly; unsuccessfully, she might add.

Shadows darkened behind her eyelids. When she opened them, she caught something out of the corner of her eye that made her stop and swim to shore.

Peter was already there.

A structure sat high in the treetops resembling the treehouses at Hangman's Tree, but this was rotting, falling apart and blanketed in moss and vines. Nets hung around it, long frayed, holes beyond repair shredded to bits. Jane stepped out of the river, avoiding the half-buried items strewn around the site. As tough as her bare feet were, they were no match for things like glass and splinters and sharp metals.

The Lost Boys soon joined them, but Peter was already investigating the building and the jagged rock formations surrounding it. Jane followed, far warier than him. This was a place of ghosts and memories. Nothing seemed scarier.

Jane looked around and noticed the monkeys in the trees. Even they stayed away from this place, staring at them from a distance.

The Lost Boys followed after Peter without Jane's caution. Reluctant though she was, Jane trotted after. Slightly waited for her, raising an eyebrow at her hesitance.

"You alright, Jane?" he asked.

"I'm fine," she insisted.

Entering the ring of tooth-like rocks on the edge of the structure where a whole wall was dangling from the branches, Jane saw Peter standing over the body of a jaguar long dead. The smell hit her with such intensity she barely suppressed the urge to vomit. The kid who'd worn the warthog mask didn't have such control over his gag reflex.

As Peter inspected the jaguar corpse, Jane noticed the monkeys again. Why were they so far away? Typically, they were bold enough to come so close as to pickpocket unsuspecting Lost Boys, or even throw nasty things at them. But these ones, they were too distant, too watchful, too scared.

The rock formation was peculiar, with its twisting sides and dark pockets, each one pointed to the sky. Jane felt as if she were standing in the mouth of a crocodile with cavities. Then there were the nets boarding the treehouse as if they used to be there for safety in case someone fell. But it was all wrong. Ropes were tied to the wrong branches. Bits and pieces hung from the trees with no apparent attachment. Gleams of metal caught her eye, but again, it was all in the wrong places. If she were to design a structure, this wasn't how she'd build it. It was no wonder it was falling apart.

Yet it was so familiar.

"Ace, come here," Peter beckoned the boy with the small nose. "Help me take a look—"

She saw the shafts first.

"GET DOWN!" Jane yelled, throwing herself on top of the onyx skinned boy.

She didn't have time to look up before she heard the trigger and the whoosh of arrows flying overhead. The boy was in such shock he didn't even squirm under her. There was a scream, she wasn't sure who. Two more waves of arrows cut through the air from the holes in the rocks, a trap even a jaguar couldn't escape from.

● ● ●

Jane looked up after the third sweep, afraid of what she'd find. The small nosed boy, Ace, lay clutching his leg where an arrow was lodged in his calf through and through. Peter held him down. Slightly peaked from behind one of the rocks, shock all over his face. When Jane saw Curly, her stomach clenched. He lay on his back right on top of one of the ropes; an obvious trigger.

Risking running straight through another wave of arrows, Jane shot up and raced to him as he started to get up. The rope released. Jane snatched it before the net of shrapnel could fall on Curly, but she doubted it would hold.

"Move," she barked, arms straining against the weight.

Curly looked at her stupidly, eyes glued on the rope in her hand. Then he saw the metal bits above him.

"Move, you bumbling stupid oaf!" Jane yelled, aggravated.

Finally coming to whatever wits he had, Curly scrambled away as fast as he could. Unable to hold much longer, and right as both Peter and Slightly were getting up to help, Jane released the rope and leapt away as the net and all its sharp contents fell.

Something hit her in the chest, taking her breath away.

Everyone hit the dirt again as more arrows flew. Lying on her back, Jane clutched the shaft protruding from her chest, gasping for breath. Then all fell silent.

Monkeys interrupted the heavy waiting stillness with screams from the distance. Realizing the trap had finally finished its course, Jane heard the Lost Boys scrambling around her, probably noticing the arrow in her chest.

• • •

"Jane!" she heard Peter cry.

Before anyone could reach her, she pulled the arrow free and felt something snap from her neck. Still gasping, still surprised to be alive, Jane stared at the arrowhead where it'd lodged itself in the wood pendant she'd worn as long as she could remember.

Lucky, she thought to herself. *I should've died.*

Peter appeared above her, an incredulous look on his face. For the first time since she'd known him, Peter Pan was speechless. He helped her up, even though the spot on her chest where the arrow had hit throbbed in protest. Blinking back tears, Jane noticed the Lost Boys around her were frozen in shock.

Then all of it broke loose.

"Yahoo!" Slightly exclaimed, leaping into the air and tucking into a flip.

The others seemed just as ecstatic, shouting and jumping and causing such an uproar that even the monkeys joined in. Jane blinked, wondering at their sudden celebration. After all, they were still in a place littered with booby-traps, and one of them still had an arrow through his calf. But Peter just grinned, keeping her balanced until she could recover.

When they were finally underway again, leaving the eerie place behind and having retrieved their things, Jane couldn't help but join in the jovial parade. She did blush fiercely, however, when Ace and Curly—who carried him because of his injury—took up a chanting song of "*Jane saved the day*" which was soon picked up by the other three.

Peter asked to see the pendant that stopped the arrow, and Jane allowed it after a moment's hesitation. He held it up to the sun, inspecting the sever now obscuring whatever used to decorate it.

"It's a nice trinket," he said at last, handing it back to her. "Who knows, maybe someday it'll be your happy thought."

Jane felt a warm glow fill her chest despite the pain. He really thought she could fly one day? Wouldn't that be something... Perhaps he was right. She clutched the pendant tightly in hand, allowing the dream to formulate in her mind.

It was the second time Jane really wanted to tell Peter everything. But tell him what? What was it she had to keep secret?

That's when the panic hit her.

I don't remember.

CHAPTER TEN
TICK TOCK

Jack was seriously considering if he could eat his makeshift staff without choking on splinters.

It had been another night of nothing to eat and hardly any sleep. He'd come to the point where he simply sat dumbly on the jungle floor in exhaustion and stared at the rough wood in his lap hungrily. The gnawing in his stomach seemed a natural now, an aggravating consistent ache.

How much do I really need a weapon, Jack debated, *if I'm going to die of hunger anyway.*

The branch's chances weren't looking so good.

About to take a bite out of his staff, his ears perked at the sound of a struggle in the underbrush. His staff didn't look so appetizing now that he was alert.

Jack shuffled to his feet as quietly as he could. Sneaking forward, he was glad for the first time that the jungle was so loud. It meant no one could hear his clumsy footsteps.

The voices reached him before he could see their sources.

"Who would 'a thought it, Bill Jukes," a ruddy and broken voice exclaimed with a cackle. "Who would 'a thought, us grabbing a filthy lost bloke!"

"The Captain will be mighty pleased, Noodles; mighty pleased indeed," another voice said, this one much deeper and hardier than the last.

Jack heard a muffled moan growl in protest. He wasn't sure if it was human or animal. Noodles gave a sharp cry in pain—at least he assumed it was Noodles; *who names their poor kid Noodles?* —followed by the heavy groan of Bill Jukes.

"Blimey; he bit me!"

"Told you we should've bound him tighter," Bill Jukes' voice was strained and squeaky.

Picking through the underbrush and trying to avoid jerking from the leaves tickling his neck, Jack saw them at last. His gut churned.

Pirates.

Bill Jukes was short and beefy with a bald head and twitchy eye. A thick black mustache hung over a sinister sneer with a gold tooth. His sleek scalp and massive arms were covered in an assortment of tattoos that made Jack cringe. A cutlass was strapped to his side.

Noodles was almost polar opposite: tall and lean with hair like straw and a gold hoop hung through his ear. He also had a gold tooth, though his looked like it was shoved in forcefully. There were two pistols at each hip, obviously well taken care of.

There was a third member of the group, though he looked more of a captive. A skinny boy, maybe twelve, with muddy hair and nut brown eyes sat there with hands and feet bound and a gag stuffed in his mouth. He did not look happy.

Noodles nursed his bleeding hand, whilst Bill Jukes had keeled over from an injury even Jack felt bad about. Their captive was roughly thrust aside, squirming on the jungle floor.

"You tighten his bonds this time," Bill Jukes heaved out, stumbling.

Noodles grumbled to himself as he hobbled over to the boy. He was bit twice more and kicked once before he could get the kid to hold still enough. Bill Jukes plopped down on a nearby rock to recover. He was so close to Jack he could smell the pirate's foul stench far too well.

"Get that Lost Boy in check," Bill Jukes growled.

Jack felt so stupid he could slap himself. Of course the kid was a Lost Boy! But he was of no use to him being captured by pirates. Somehow, Jack had to get the kid away. The plan began to hatch sooner than he expected; a risky, insane plan, but it could work.

He was so glad he hadn't eaten his staff.

Hefting the branch, Jack tried to advance through the jungle underbrush without causing too much rustling. He prayed the pirates were as stupid as he hoped. At least they didn't hear the faint crunch of his footsteps as he approached an unsuspecting Bill Jukes.

Lifting his staff to his shoulder, Jack prepared to give the blow.

His stomach chose that moment to growl.

Blast it!

Bill Jukes whirled around. "What—?"

Jack swung and smashed his staff against the pirate's tattooed head before he could finish. The pirate looked at him dumbly, eye twitching with surreal speed. Jack wacked him again. This time, Bill Jukes collapsed unconscious.

Before he could heft his branch again, Noodles turned right in front of him. Jack panicked and socked him in the nose. Hands covering his swelling schnoz, the pirate wailed in such anger, confusion, and pain that Jack almost felt bad about thwacking him in the side of the head with a tree branch. He did it anyway.

His heart raced with exhilaration when Noodles crumpled and didn't get up. His plan had gone surprisingly well. Who would 'a thought it?

The Lost Boy stared at him, eyes wide.

"If I take the gag off," Jack questioned as he crouched beside him, "will you bite me?"

The boy sat stunned for a moment as if contemplating his response. He shook his head.

"Glad we've got that straight."

Jack took the gag off the boy's mouth. As agreed, the Lost Boy didn't bite him. But he didn't talk after the gag had been removed, either. As Jack went on to untie the kid's bounds, a low growl behind him made his heart drop. Turning around cautiously, he met a familiar face: his old friend, the cougar.

"*Blasted bloody…*" he grumbled, hefting his staff once more and standing protectively over the boy.

The cougar narrowed her eyes. Peeling her lips back, she yowled. This time, Jack didn't jump or run. Because this time he had someone else to think about. He didn't know the kid, probably barely avoided getting bit by the kid, but he did care about Wendy. If this boy was a friend of hers, then Jack would do everything within his power to protect him.

The cougar stepped over the sleeping body of Bill Jukes lightly. Jack bent his knees, tightened his grip on his staff. In one instant, she pounced and his instincts kicked into high gear. He bashed his staff at the cougar, throwing her to the ground sprawling.

She hissed angrily at him and went for a second attack. Dropping to a crouch, Jack struck her in the chest as she jumped over him. An explosion of pain raked down his back, then came back tenfold in two additional swipes of fire. Jack cried out. Whipping around, he smashed his staff against the cougar's head. She yowled, retreating. Whacking her muzzle with her paw agitatedly, she turned and fled into the jungle.

Jack stood, breathing heavy, completely stunned.

With more of a groan than a sneer, Jack growled, "Bad kitty."

Back searing in pain and sweat sliding down his face, he turned to find the Lost Boy standing behind him. Somehow, the kid had wrestled free from his bonds. He probably had plenty of opportunity to escape, yet he was still here.

"You... you fought that," he blinked, "all by yourself."

Jack furrowed his eyebrows, looked around as if maybe he was talking to someone else. "Yeah, I guess I did."

Still completely shocked, the kid added, "And you won."

"That part's confusing me, too," Jack admitted.

"You saved me?"

"Twice, but who's counting?"

The kid's face screwed up in suspicion. "Are you a tribesman?"

"Do I *look* like a Native Neverlandian to you?"

He shrugged. "No, I guess not."

Jack studied the boy's face, hoping this venture would pay off. Another wave of fire hit his back like a shadow of the attack. He hissed in pain, gasping for breath. He looked at the kid again.

"What's your name?"

"Nibs," the boy said, standing straighter, "loyal follower of Peter Pan and one of the original Lost Boys."

"Nice to meet you, Nibs. I'm Jack." He tried to smile, but it wasn't quite working the way he wanted it to. "And I, uh, I need to ask you a few things. First... do you have food?"

Nibs shook his head. "I don't have any on me, but I can help you find some."

"Great!" Jack exclaimed in relief. "Secondly, where can I find Hangman's Tree?"

*****

Jane stood in front of the mirror, examining the circular web of a bruise in the center of her breastbone. It looked worse than it felt, or at least that's what she told those who asked. Not that she'd let anyone else actually see it. There were some instances in which she had to remind everyone that she was, in fact, still a girl.

She made the mistake of touching it right in its gaudy yellow center, hissing a curse as fire shot down the sensitive wound. The bruise flowered into royal purple before creating a ring of black and blue. Aye, it was somewhat small with a diameter nearly the length of her thumb, but it gave a nasty bight.

The pendant that saved her life sat on a table beside her, its face completely obscured from the arrowhead's blow. She couldn't even remember what was on it before. Had it been important?

Shaking her head, she pulled her shirt on over her head and looked in the mirror again. What was it she was supposed to remember? She knew she should keep trying, knew that perhaps if she thought long enough then maybe she would know what it was that filled her with such dread to tell Peter. But why wouldn't she tell Peter?

Agh, this is making my head hurt!

Pulling her hair up, Jane stepped out onto the balcony where a rope bridge connected her treehouse to Peter's. The cool evening breeze blew against her face pleasantly. The stars, the really bright ones, were beginning to shine through the sunset amongst the moons. Closing her eyes, she walked out on the rope bridge and felt it sway beneath her feet. Like this, she could almost believe she was on the sea. She wasn't sure why the ocean always seemed to await her in her dreams, but it was always there when she closed her eyes. The ocean, and Peter Pan.

"I can see you're recovering nicely."

Jane turned to find Peter walking towards her as if he'd stepped out of the starlight. Her ears grew hot.

"It's just a bruise," she insisted. "It'll heal."

"That's good to hear." His eyes glittered mischievously, hands held behind his back. "I have a surprise for you."

She raised her eyebrows, pleasantly suspicious.

With an air of extravagance, Peter produced a mask from behind his back, a distressed gold in color with ebony spots. She gasped, overcome with joy.

"It's a leopard," he explained. "The boys and I thought that, after what happened earlier, you deserved it."

"So, as a symbol of a rotting corpse?" Jane asked teasingly.

Peter shook his head. "Nah, just as a reminder of the day you truly became a Lost Girl."

Jane looked up at him in shock. "Really?"

• • •

"Really."

Such a glow filled her it left her speechless.

Peter laughed. "Go on, take it; it's yours."

Jane did, holding it as if it were a dream in her hands that could vaporize at any moment. The carving was elegantly done, and that combined with the paint made it look graceful yet dangerous. She felt so incredibly... happy. So happy she felt she could fly.

"What's that?"

Jane turned her head to see what he was looking at. "What's what?"

"Not there." Peter raised his hand and touched her neck, making her skin tingle. "Here."

By the expression on his face, she grew concerned. "Is it a tick?"

"No, it's a drawing."

"A drawing?"

"A clock," he explained, fingers brushing a spot behind her ear, "tattooed right by your hairline."

"Why would I have a clock on my neck?" Jane asked, growing more concerned.

"You don't remember?" Peter pulled back, looking into her face.

"I don't..." Her mind raced. "I don't think so."

He gave her a sympathetic look. She didn't usually like that look, but on Peter she didn't mind so much. Still, Jane couldn't help but feel that confusing dread coming back to her.

"So, some of the boys were going to play a game of tribesmen and pirates," he started, changing the subject. "You want to join?"

"Not tonight," she said, still lost in thought. "I'm not up for it."

"Alright, maybe next time, then," he offered, already disappearing again.

"Yeah, maybe next... time..."

Time.

It hit her in a rush.

Peter was wrong. The leopard mask, it wasn't a symbol of her becoming a Lost Girl. It was a warning, a trap. And she hated herself for it.

She wished she'd never remembered.

CHAPTER ELEVEN
PLEASE BELIEVE

"Alice! Alice!"

Alice spun around quickly at the sound of her name, nearly swatting some fairies in her haste. Thankfully, no one got hurt, though some rang angrily at her. Alice just finished stammering a few apologies when Hazel caught up to her in a streak of pixie dust. Before she said anything, Alice offered her hand for the tired fairy to sit. Hazel gratefully obliged.

"What is it?"

"Tink's just arrived," Hazel gasped out, breathing faster than a rocking-horsefly. "You have to... You have to come and tell her what you told me you needed to tell her. We should hurry!"

Alice felt a surge of anxiousness. "Where is she?"

"At the entrance. Dandelion's bustling over her and Myrtle's asking her all sorts of questions."

Without another word, Alice cut through the garden as fast as she dared, splashing through the pond and jumping over flowerbeds. Hazel quickly leapt up and latched onto her braid to stay with her. A few angry jingles and hasty apologies later, Alice arrived at the cave entrance quickly enough.

She noticed Hazel fly wobbly ahead, as if terribly dizzy.

"Sorry," Alice said guiltily. "Are you alright?"

"Who, *me*?" Hazel waved it off. "I'm fine. Oops!" She seemed to trip in midair, but caught herself.

• • •

A flurry of fairies zipped around in an excited cocoon of pixie dust and bells. But Alice didn't need to look twice before she found the returned fairy.

Tinker Bell's wings were long and strong, illuminating a golden aura much brighter than the others'. Short yellow hair was tied up, but there was no keeping back those thick bangs. Her eyes were grey flecked with gold, filled with a thirst and hardness that only came from adventure. With a vine wrapped around her waist and hardy bark boots up to her knees, she seemed ready for one.

There was a split second when those grey eyes met hers before the fairy zoomed right up to Alice's face.

"Who are you?" Tink inquired instantly, the bells behind her voice sharp. "How do you know me? Where did you come from? How did you get here?"

Blinking in surprise, Alice backed up a step so Tink wasn't right on her nose. "My name's Alice Pleasance Liddell from England—err, Wonderland."

Tink narrowed her eyes. "What's a Mainland girl from Wonderland doing in Neverland?"

"Uh…" Alice hesitated. "That's not the point."

She held her breath when Tink held a dagger up to her eyelashes. "It is if you value your sense of sight!" the fairy countered.

"Calm down!" Alice protested. "I'm here to find the Queen of Hearts' master, some kind of ultimate evil planning a war and somehow tricked my friends and me into coming to different worlds. I don't know who; I don't know where; I don't know why. All I know is that *someone* wants us, they're planning a war, and we need to stop them. I came to either retrieve more information or take this hidden wraith down."

She waited, breathless, completely aware that she'd said too much, even more aware that it couldn't possibly be convincing.

Tink glared at her, that dagger still far too close for comfort. Then she scowled, backing away and strapping the knife to her leg. Alice heaved a sigh of relief. Hazel hovered close by, visibly baffled. She almost forgot she hadn't told the fairy the reason she was in Neverland.

"Fine, I believe you," Tinker Bell huffed. "I've heard wind of a strange evil rising from the depths during my recent travels, collecting dangerous followers from different worlds to build an army. But you still haven't answered all my questions. How'd you get here?"

"Using this."

She took the pocket watch out from under her shirt. Holding it out for them to see, Alice noticed the soft chime of gasps she'd grown very used to. A few pixies fluttered closer. Only Tink, Hazel, and Sparrow, who seemed to have appeared out of nowhere, ventured close enough to touch it.

Tinker Bell traced the edge of the silver cover. "Where did you get this?"

"A friend," Alice said simply as she tucked the watch under her shirt again. "We used it to bring us from Wonderland to Neverland, though we didn't know where we'd end up."

"*We?*" Tink's fingers hovered over the dagger strapped to her leg. "How many are you?"

"Five, all from... the Mainland," she explained, using the peculiar word Tink had used. "We got separated when fleeing from the dragon on Neverpeak Mountain."

Raising an eyebrow in suspicion, the fairy asked curiously, "How did you know about me?"

Alice bit her lip, realizing only then that this was the difficult part. "Because my friend told me about you... Wendy Darling."

Tink's face grew scarlet in fury, flying right in her face again. "DO NOT *LIE* TO ME! I've searched *everywhere*, broke through the wall between worlds *countless* times, for over a *year*! Peter's Shadow hasn't returned. The only probable reason why it's taking so long, why no one has found *anything*, is that she's gone! WENDY DARLING IS *DEAD*!"

Tink's throat choked up in tears, unable to shout again with any fraction of composure.

Alice waited patiently for her to calm down. She didn't blame the fairy for being angry. She knew exactly what it felt like to think someone she loved and cared about was as good as dead. That feeling of complete hopelessness, helplessness, with no reason to expect anything to change for the better; oh, Alice knew that feeling all too well.

But then she'd met Wendy, a girl who was in practically the same situation as her, maybe even a worse one. But Wendy had given her reason to hope again, be happy again, *live* again. Because of that, Alice wasn't sure she ever would've been able to survive that Facility, not to mention save Remus.

Now she had the chance to give that hope to someone else.

● ● ●

Tink sniffed, rubbing her nose. Her face struggled between anger and grief.

Hazel put a hand on her friend's arm. "Tink, trust me."

Hesitantly, Sparrow placed a comforting arm around her tense shoulders. Tink's lip quivered. Tears streamed down her cheeks. But she remained silent.

Hazel turned to Alice, nodding encouragingly. "Go on, Alice. Tell her what you told me."

Alice sat in the grass and waited for the three pixies to take a seat on her knees before she began. She explained just about everything. First, she relayed everything she knew about Wendy being kidnapped, not killed, by Hook and taken back to England where she escaped, fleeing to London. She followed up with a brief explanation about the Facility and how they'd also kidnapped Wendy when her parents refused to send her away.

When she told them about how the Facility was underground, she could tell when the confusion cleared up in Tink's eyes. It was the perfect explanation for why the pixie hadn't found her. Alice didn't give very many details about Wonderland and their adventures there, but the fairies got the point.

When she had finished, Tinker Bell's light glowed ever brighter.

Wiping away stray tears, the fairy hopped to her feet in a sudden burst of confidence. "We need to get you to Hangman's Tree right away!"

"Are you going right now?" Sparrow asked as Tink fluttered up excitedly.

"Of course," Tink exclaimed as Hazel flew up to join her. "Peter needs to hear this as soon as possible!"

"Aren't you coming, Sparrow?" Hazel asked.

His olive green eyes flicked from Hazel's doe eyes to Tink's gold flecked ones. The overjoyed pixie had stopped her bouncy flight to hover in place as she waited for Sparrow's response. He seemed hesitant. Alice raised an eyebrow when he saw Tink's face, the resolution settling on his own.

She wasn't surprised when Sparrow nodded. "It's about time I joined you on one of your adventures."

*****

Jane moved carefully, picking her way through the jungle. She tried her best to keep an eye on him, but he'd escaped from sight when she had her back turned for but a split second. Thankfully she knew a bit about tracking, though if Pan decided to fly she'd be in trouble.

There was a nagging question in the back of her mind, a nuisance really, questioning why she still did this. She didn't have to. She could just live for the moment, be a Lost Girl, have a family in the Lost Boys, stay with Peter.

Blast it; don't fall in love with that boy!

Besides, Peter Pan was never hers. He never would be.

But couldn't she just forget again? Wasn't she happiest when she didn't remember?

Ah, but that's just it! I did remember. Didn't I see to that when I got that bloody clock on my neck?

And that was truly the most painful part of it all. She'd made her choice, seen to every possibility except for regret. In a way, even that part she'd taken care of. As soon as she'd stepped onto the sandy shores of Neverland, as soon as she took Pan's hand, there really was no going back from this.

A voice pricked her ears, one she knew instantly to be Pan's. She almost walked in on them, but hid herself quickly behind a tree before she could be noticed. Lowering her breathing, she waited, listened.

Peter was talking to Tootles.

"We need to accept it," his voice cracked. "She's not coming back."

"No, no, *no!*"

Jane nearly jumped and almost gave up her position. She'd never heard Tootles speak before. She's always assumed he was a selective mute. And she never would've expected him to speak with such volume.

"SHE'S NOT DEAD!" Tootles shouted, a voice so pained and shocked and *childlike* that Jane bit back her instant heartache. "You have to believe; you've *got* to believe! You can't give up on her. *You* of *all* people—"

"What other choice do I have?!" Peter proclaimed, the hurt in his voice a thousand times worse. "My Shadow hasn't returned; Tink's come back empty handed. Even she's lost all hope. What am I supposed to do?"

"*Believe*, Peter!" Tootles insisted desperately. "You *have* to believe. You've *got* to have faith."

"Faith?"

"You're Peter Pan!"

"That doesn't mean anything."

"It means everything!"

"Not anymore…"

"That's a stupid—"

"I CAN'T *FLY* ANYMORE!"

It was as if Neverland itself recoiled at those words. Jane's heart pounded loudly in the stretching silence. Peter Pan... couldn't fly anymore? The possibility was beyond even her understanding. He strived off of belief, always had faith, *that* was the Peter Pan she knew in spite of everything else she discovered that contradicted what she'd been taught. *That* was what made him remarkable. *That* was what made him dangerous. *That* was what made him fly.

A long time ago when she was just a little girl, Jane was told that the day Peter Pan stopped believing, the day he couldn't fly, it would be the end of all of Neverland. In a way, perhaps it held truth. Jane didn't think such a place could survive without faith.

Despite all previous battles of identity and moral, Jane felt her heart break.

She heard Peter sigh, completely defeated. "I can't. I've tried and I can't. I don't have any faith left."

"But Wendy would," Tootles persisted, voice frighteningly low and unnatural for a child. "If she was in your stead, *she* would believe. How can you say you loved her?"

Jane felt the electrical charge and ozone concentration change in the air as Pan was thrown back into a passion. "I LOVED HER MORE THAN ANYONE!"

"THEN *PROVE IT!*" Tootles shouted. "Don't give up on her. She would *never* give up on any of us, especially you."

Jane peaked behind the tree just in time to see Tootles turn on his heal and scamper off into the jungle. Peter's stiff posture fell away when he collapsed on the ground, back towards her. She was startled when she heard him cry.

A mix of emotions stirred in her, creating a panic. Such fear, such sympathy, such sorrow at seeing him, such anger at herself. She could stop this. She could leave. She could stay. She could tell him. She could fix his broken heart, but it could also shatter her own...

Throat knotted, unable to hold back her own tears, she turned and fled.

CHAPTER TWELVE
GHOSTS

The pain didn't subside, but Kai had begun to get so used to the throbbing in his ankle that he was as numb to it as he was to his foot. When he moved the wrong way and his shirt rubbed against his ribs, the wound there would sting in a rage. Hopefully it wasn't infected.

Under his feet the water sped by in a haze. Exhaustion had him in its grasp. Emptiness hollowed his stomach with too much familiarity.

Then the scene beyond his toes changed to white crested waves and then a stretch of sand. With a lurch, the creature dropped him.

Kai twisted unnaturally to avoid hitting his head, but regret surged as soon as he landed. Fire shot up his ankle. Sand clung to his wound agitatedly. Every muscle aching, Kai lay completely still on his side, breathing heavy, staring at the shoreline.

He heard the creature who'd taken him from the mermaids before he saw it, great claps of beating back the wind above him. Then the creature came into view, a descending white blur at first but quickly taking shape. The bird turned her long, graceful neck to look back at him. Pink feathers framed her eyes and inked down her throat. Wispy curls of feathers grew through her wings and tail, giving her an angelic aura in the sunlight.

The bird walked toward him on stork-like pearly legs, seeming to grow ever bigger as she drew nearer until she proved taller than a horse directly beside him. Kai blinked up at it, still comprehending.

● ● ●

"*Tusen tack,*" Kai muttered, his voice terribly broken.

The bird bowed her head, nibbling the toe of his left boot. Kai looked down toward it, noting the unnatural angle of his foot with a grimace.

Dislocated, he discerned in dismay.

Straightening herself, the bird took to the air with a leap and a flutter. Kai expected her to fly off, but instead she landed on a beached old dingey, pick framed eyes staring right at him. He lifted his head out of the sand awkwardly. Did the bird want him to follow her? Stranger things had happened to him.

"I can't," he called, gesturing to his awry foot. The movement caused sand to rub against his wound again. Besides, the weathered old skeleton would never last on water anymore.

The bird gave out a high cry like a pipe. Turning away, she extended her wings and fanned her wispy tail of curled feathers. The light illuminated the white to offset the pink. Then she left, flying toward Neverland's main Island which resided far across the channel.

Kai's head landed right back on the sand, exhaustion, pain, and hunger pulsing through him. His ankle seemed a thousand times worse since he saw it. He knew he needed to set it. The only problem was: with what?

It hit him like a rock. *The boat.*

Before he could overthink it, Kai rolled over and began crawling by his elbows toward the dingey. Pain shot up his ankle with every jostling movement. Biting it back, Kai closed the distance quickly.

He used his stolen knife when he could, cutting the torn sail off its broken mast and ripping it to strips. After close examination, Kai broke off the least splintered board he could find and split it in two over his knee. Heaving, he sat up in the sand and braced himself for the painful part.

Kai tried to think of any instance in which he'd had to do this, but fixing dislocation... he'd only ever witnessed it. He remembered helping Gerda's father with a few house calls back in his home village, Anders. There was one instance where he'd helped the doctor with holding down a patient who'd dislocated his knee after an accident with a horse and a tree. That seemed so long ago, now. But a dislocated ankle couldn't be too different from a dislocated knee, could it?

Tenderly feeling where the bones separated, Kai readied himself. He took a deep breath. With terrible, agonizing rolling, he eased his heel down and around. There was a snap, bursting pain flaring as his ankle popped back in socket. He hissed a curse in Swedish, breathing heavily.

Gritting his teeth, Kai took the two halves of broken board and held them up on either side of his foot. He quickly wrapped his foot and shin with the strips of sail to bind the boards in place. Splint completed, Kai fell back exhaustedly to wait out the pain.

When he opened his eyes, he saw it: the massive skull shaped rock formation looming over and behind him. His skin crawled. Someone was watching him.

*****

"Why'd you call her that if it's not her name?" Nibs asked, adding to the stream of questions he'd been rattling off.

"Her initials," Jack explained, not minding the questions so much as the throbbing pain in his back. "R. E.

D. Red. I'm not sure why she's called it. I never really thought to ask; she doesn't like talking about her history. But I guess I shouldn't bother her about it. Everyone calls her Red."

"If you ask me, I'd think maybe if you called her something else, it'd be more uplifting than some acronym," Nibs suggested.

"How'd you get to that assumption?"

"Well, I don't know much about girls or anything. But I do know a good lot about Lost Boys. None of them are too open about their pasts when they come to Neverland. That's fine enough; Neverland's supposed to be an escape from all that. But it's not always so easy. Most boys need a little help getting adjusted to having others love them again, even if it's just calling them by name. There's a lot of power in a name, you know." Nibs paused a moment before adding, "Sometimes all you need is to be remembered, especially in a place where it's so easy to forget."

Jack pondered that, realizing how right Nibs was. He'd felt the same way most of his life though he never really knew it until now. As a child, he'd had his own band of lost children. Orphans could be just like Lost Boys, in a sense, even if they didn't have a boat to take them to Neverland. They had to build their own place of refuge.

"How'd you get to be so wise?" Jack questioned with a raised eyebrow.

Nibs smirked. "I happen to be much older than you think."

"How much older?"

"In Mainland years, very much older than twelve."

"Very helpful."

Nibs laughed, a sound like hiccups. "Honestly, I don't even know. Time's so different here in Neverland. It hardly ever exists, and when it does it's completely irregular. There's no point trying to keep record of... of... *years*, when they only live in the Mainland."

"You could've simply said you didn't want to tell me how old you are."

There was a rush of leaves and a long body fell down right in front of Jack's face. Jumping back in surprise, he swore loudly, nearly tripping over roots. The dangling snake stared at him, flicking its tongue.

A shiver ran down Jack's spine. "Agh, I *hate* snakes."

Of course, the kid laughed at him and, to his astonishment, plucked the long snake from the tree to rest on his arms. "You're afraid of old Kaa? He's so lazy, he wouldn't hurt a fly!"

"You *named* that thing?" Jack frowned, repulsed.

"Sure, when something becomes recognizable, you tend to name it." Nibs shrugged, holding the snake out towards him.

Jack flinched back. "Don't you dare!"

"Relax," he assured, letting the lazy snake slither away into the undergrowth. "I'm almost certain Kaa would get hurt if you laid a hand on him."

"You've got that right," Jack grumbled, realizing his back had begun to bleed again. "Why do you call it that, anyway?"

"A story. Well, except *that* Kaa was a huge, beast eating python. *This* Kaa isn't really that huge, and he's way too lazy to eat large live animals."

Not that huge? He'd beg to differ.

● ● ●

"Who told you that story?" Jack asked before thinking. He shook his head. "Ah, never mind, I think I know."

Nibs turned back to him slowly. "You do?"

"Well, yeah. It was Wendy, wasn't it? It makes sense."

"How do you know about Wendy?" the kid asked warily in a way that made it seem like he would scamper off at any moment.

Jack frowned. "I didn't tell you?"

Nibs just narrowed his eyes suspiciously.

"Guess I didn't… Anyway, Wendy's a friend of mine; she was with me when we arrived here. We got separated at some—"

"You're lying! That can't be possible."

"Lying? I'm not lying; I'm the one who told you about Wendy, remember?"

"Prove it!" Nibs demanded, backing up a step. "Tell me her full name! Tell me how she can't have been killed. Tell me why Peter's Shadow hasn't come back."

"Look, I don't know anything about a shadow or Wendy dying. That's all news to me, and personally, I don't think she's anymore dead than you and me."

"Prove it!"

"Blast it, kid, I can't exactly prove anything without her here!" Jack exclaimed. "She's not dead, she was just kidnapped. The Hook pirate took her to England, which was a pretty stupid idea on his part, and she escaped but was kidnapped *again* by some maniac Facility that wants kids who've experienced magic—including me, unfortunately. That's where I met Wendy, and Red and Kai; and Wendy introduced us to Alice who, thanks to this random woman, led us all to Wonderland where we battled the bloody Queen of Hearts that somehow or another sent us on this ridiculous quest to find some evil mastermind who no one knows who in the bloody world it is! Then old Long Ears sent us to Neverland where we got separated not ten minutes into being here, and after getting my back shredded by a cougar, I have to try to convince *you* that this crazy story is true!"

"What's her name?"

"Whose?"

"Wendy's."

"What bloody good would that prove; she goes around introducing herself as Wendy Moira Angela Darling to everyone she meets!"

Nibs' expression shifted. "Wendy's alive?"

"Unless I've been seeing a ghost for nearly half a year, then I think we've settled that."

The kid wasn't listening, his face brightening by the second. "Wendy's alive!"

Whooping in delight, Nibs flew straight up in the air, doing flips in his joy. Jack gaped in astonishment. He'd heard that the Lost Boys could fly, but seeing it was a whole different experience. The only time he'd ever seen anyone fly was when a jubjub bird nearly took Alice for a ride back in Wonderland. He didn't think that counted, though.

As soon as Nibs landed back on the ground, he grabbed Jack's wrist and began dragging him through the jungle with new exhilaration. "We need to get you to Hangman's Tree right away!"

"Whoa, slow down," Jack cried. "Not everyone here can fly, you know!"

*****

Kai couldn't help but stare, still getting adjusted to the crawling sense of being watched by the dead. It was all he could do with nowhere to run and no way to fight.

The ghost was shrouded in a cloak of thin mist, enough to reveal she didn't belong to this life anymore but also enough to show how she was when she had. Beauty clung to her, though faded an undistinguished. Sharp yet fair features complimented her dark mess of curls and rich brown eyes. By her layered skirts and rustic corset, Kai discerned she must've been a pirate. But she seemed so... young. Not a child, but certainly not much older than twenty.

But her eyes held a gleam suggesting she could see farther than the living could ever fathom. That in itself unnerved Kai above all.

In a blink, the ghost was directly before him. With a start, Kai shuffled back, pain jolting down his ankle at the movement. The ghost didn't flinch, even as he hissed a curse. His throat felt dry. His heart pounded. With a grace so *inhuman*, the ghost knelt next to him, the edge of her skirt passing through Kai's hand. A shock of suffocating cold bit through skin and bone, and a memory that didn't belong to him flashed behind his eyelids:

A cradle in a dim room, fallen over and empty of a child that should've been inside.

Breathing heavily, Kai noticed the thin layer of frost on his knuckles. He'd felt worse things, colder things before. But the unfamiliar image confused him.

The ghost furrowed her brow, eyes searching his face. She reached up toward his face slowly. He wanted to pull away. But the ocean washed up around him and he realized he had nowhere to run. Fingertips lightly brushed his jaw, a sharp spark jolting down his scar like lightening.

"*Blodig—!*" Kai exclaimed, jerking away from the ghost.

She gasped, staring at her hand strangely.

Shifting away from her, Kai demanded, "What do you want?"

"You felt it, too?" the ghost spoke, ignoring his question.

Kai scowled, mind racing. He couldn't discern if the ghost was hostile or not. She could obviously hurt him, despite her lack of solidity. But he couldn't fight her, and he couldn't run.

"You have something," the ghost muttered, pointing to her own jaw in an imitation of Kai's scar. "It repels magic, yet is made of it."

Gritting his teeth, Kai tried to ignore the ringing tremor beneath his scar.

The ghost placed her hands in her lap and leaned forward. "Who are you?"

"Why would I tell you?"

"Because I'll find out whether you tell me or not," she replied without any break in expression. "This way is easier and the least painful for you."

His stomach tightened. "Kai."

She nodded slightly, vaguely staring at the ocean turf. "I was once called Sylvia... but that was a long time ago."

"*AGH!*"

Kai sprang to his feet, drew his dagger. Pain shot down his ankle. A large fog came barreling towards him, transparent cutlass raised. Kai barely had time to cover his head in defense before the ghost shot straight through him. Chill sucked away his breath. Daggers split down his scar, ripping his soul. Fragments of images he'd never seen before flashed through his mind:

A toy bear laying forgotten on a leafy floor.

Swords clashing. Gunfire blaring.

A touch on the cheek in parting, never to see them again.

Kai fell to his knees shivering, clutching his chest as if he could catch his breath in his hands.

"Long John, stop!"

Kai glanced up to find Sylvia placed in front of him, barring the other ghost from advancing. Even so, the other ghost growled in pain, clawing at his collarbone and leaning heavily on a crutch under his left arm.

"Let me at 'im!" he roared. "Show 'em not to go trespassing again. Let's see how his soul handles another—"

"No."

"He *reeks* of Lost Boy. You shouldn't defend him, Sylvia. His kind put us on this bloody rock. His kind should be the ones trapped on the other side of death."

"After everything that's happened, do you still think you can make that judgement?"

"Don't give me that moral crap; we're beyond that by now."

"Have you forgotten everything?" Sylvia shot. "The battle; the curse; Jim?"

The ghost grew grave, his aggressive posture melting, scowl deepening. "I forget nothing. Especially not..." He shook his head and pinched the bridge of his nose. Kai measured him up, taking in the missing left leg and thick

● ● ●

crutch. When the ghost cast a sideways glance at him, Kai felt his muscles relax. There would be no attack.

The ghost turned back to Sylvia. "Why is he here?"

"The Neverbird brought him."

"That wasn't smart," he huffed. "That bird's losing her bloody mind..."

"I think he can save us."

Kai felt his stomach tighten. He'd heard those words before. He didn't like those words and the disappointment that followed.

The ghost, Long John, sighed, "Seems you're losing your mind, too."

"He has something," Sylvia insisted, "a sliver of magic, *strong* magic. You felt it. It could free us."

"No such power lies in Neverland, save for the bleeding tribesman who cursed us," Long John growled. "And he's dead and moved on, thanks to your husband. No Lost Boy has any memory of that kind of power; we would know."

"I'm not a Lost Boy."

Both Sylvia and Long John looked back at him. Kai squared his jaw, feeling he could at last gain some leverage. In facing two potential foes who could hurt him easily, he would need whatever advantage he could get.

"What are you, then?" Long John questioned eerily. "Where are you from, if not Neverland?"

"Anders," Kai said simply before specifying, "a town in... the Mainland."

"There ain't any magic there either."

Sylvia went to respond to that, but Kai beat her to it. "No, none that I could tell. But I have been elsewhere, a land

• • •

117

ruled by ice and magic. I have witnessed magic more powerful than anything I've come across."

"It explains the scar," Sylvia added to Long John. "You *felt* it, I know."

The pirate ghost frowned between the both of them. Kai held his stare steadily, no break in expression.

With a scowl, Long John growled, "We'll discuss this later." In a manner that rivaled living mannerisms and ghostly swiftness, he stomped off with hardly a limp despite his missing leg.

Trying to control his breathing, Kai turned to the remaining ghost. Sylvia studied him with dark pools of eyes.

"Come with me," was all she said.

CHAPTER THIRTEEN
HANGMAN'S TREE

Strangely enough, there was not a Lost Boy in sight. Not one. And of all people, Wendy knew where to look. But there were no patrols, no lookouts, no hunting or raiding parties. Was it pure chance or was the Island intervening? Were they actually headed to Hangman's Tree, or did the landscape change and let them lost?

Even so, her heart kept pounding excitedly. Every step was taking her closer and closer to the Lost Boys, to Peter Pan.

I'm almost there.

Tiger Lily followed close behind them, footsteps silent and tomahawk in hand. She seemed more like the tribeswoman Wendy remembered, having left her headdress and Bagheera behind. As Tiger Lily was the only one from the Panther Tribe with them—that she was aware of—Wendy debated whether they could lose her. Was it worth the risk? By herself, perhaps she could've lost the Chieftess, especially if she could still fly. But with Red and without her happy thoughts, she wasn't so sure.

Better stick to the plan, then, she thought with a sigh. *There's no getting out of it.*

At least it was only Tiger Lily who'd come with them. Any more tribesmen and it would look like a raiding party, which would not be received well.

Red came closer, her footsteps almost as quiet as the Chieftess'. "Do you think they'll be able to find the others?" she asked in a low tone.

• • •

Wendy suppressed the instinct to admit that she honestly didn't know. The Island wasn't large, but it was certainly complicated. And even though having the Lost Boys' help would greaten their odds, it wasn't a guarantee that they'd be able to find Kai, Alice, or Jack.

Instead of admitting her concerns, she responded, "I hope so."

It was the truth. Sometimes all that can be said is faith.

Something caught her eye, a discoloration in the leafy floor. Wendy knelt to brush away the leaves, exposing a grey and black face painted dark around empty eyes. Picking it up, she recognized the raccoon mask with a smile.

"We're close," she said softly.

A buzz came through her from the bottoms of her feet, like the Island was humming in agreement. Almost as quickly, she heard it. Whistling notes traveled in the wind, so faint it could've been a distant bird song. Her heart pounded and her gut churned with a thousand butterflies.

Peter.

Like a child, Wendy ran leaping and bounding and overcome with such a feeling of being *alive* she could barely contain it. There was no regard for those following her, no regard for how childish she appeared, how ridiculous she seemed with her bubbling joy and excited laughter. The Island around her pulsed like a heartbeat, cheering her on, calling her home.

Wendy was coming home.

She broke through the underbrush and skittered to a stop. Heart racing, breathing heavy, Wendy spun around in exhilaration. The treehouses, the rope bridges, the secret

● ● ●

entrances to underground tunnels, the toys and weapons strewn about; it was almost exactly as she remembered.

"Wendy!" Red burst out of the jungle right behind her, face flushed. Then she noticed where they were. "Whoa."

Tiger Lily seemed to appear right beside her, face hard as if she did not appreciate Wendy's outburst without warning. But she didn't particularly care what the Chieftess thought. They were in Wendy's house now. That changed things.

"Where is everyone?" Red asked curiously.

Wendy lowered her eyes as she wondered the same thing. Then the music registered, pure and clear as the wind through the stars. There was no other sound like it.

"Come on," she encouraged, following the sound of panpipes.

As much as she wanted to take her time going through Hangman's Tree again, she found herself trotting through with growing anticipation. Home wasn't complete without her family.

So many memories surged through her though, especially approaching the original tree where her old house had been raised, where Peter stayed just underground. It had grown over the decades despite its being hollow. Strong now, it held strings of bridges and wraparound porches and little fairy houses, but the only treehouse was hers.

Wendy skidded to a halt right beside this tree, leaning against it, watching the clearing behind it. It was a dip in the floor, like an arena, one where they would go for gatherings or games or training. But now it was filled with dancing Lost Boys and music without unity, pounding drums and running children. Above all the noise and laughter was the panpipes that brought all the chaos together.

Wendy's heart fluttered. *There he is.*

Peter Pan. Skipping and dancing with boyish frivolity, playing his panpipes in playful serene melody. The dying sunlight, the brightest kind, glittered gold through his auburn hair. Butterflies and dragonflies buzzed around him as if attracted by Pan's music, though the surrounding boys tried to catch them.

Wendy could've watched this all day.

Tiger Lily ruined it.

"What is this?" she questioned with a frown.

"Don't you know a party when you see one?" Red responded, raising an eyebrow.

"I know it. But why celebrate?"

Wendy shrugged. "Why not?"

"They are making an uproar to rival the jungle," Tiger Lily criticized. "This is juvenile."

"Yup." Wendy grinned mischievously. "And to think, you're about to form an allegiance with them."

She didn't seem amused.

Wendy sighed, bracing herself to approach. Did she just walk in? She looked at Peter again, this time noticing the dark circles under his eyes, the droop in his shoulders, how *thin* he looked. Throat tightening, she stepped into the clearing.

She wanted to say something clever, but words seemed out of her capacity. Was she nervous? Why was she nervous? Or was it just excitement? She never could tell which sometimes.

• • •

The closest faces turned to her, then swiveled back again in frozen shock. A wave of stillness slowly came over the boys as her presence became noticed. Discomfort itched in her cheeks as mouths hung open and expressions blanked.

At the sight of one of the Twins, she moved toward him and shoved the raccoon mask in his fossilized hands. "Here, I found this outside," she said. "You really need to keep track of your things. Remember that glass eye? Don't want another incident like that."

"Wendy?"

Her heart glowed at the voice.

Excited, she decided. *That's what it is.*

Wendy turned to face him, reveling in the way he looked at her: shock, disbelief, confusion, *hope*. She tucked a curl behind her ear, a smile tugging the corner of her mouth. "Hello, Peter."

There was a breath of stillness where Neverland itself seemed to pause and watch with longing impatience, and the stars didn't blink, and the wind stilled its course, and the butterflies sat down a moment should the beat of their wings disturb the silence.

In one fell swoop, Peter Pan shattered the stillness, darting forward and colliding into her, catching her into him. The breath nearly knocked out of her. But she clasped her arms around him, burying her face in his chest. He held her tighter.

"I thought you were dead," Peter said, his jaw pressed against the top of her head. "I thought…"

"I know."

Peter swallowed hard, and Wendy knew he was fighting back tears, knew he wanted to say more but wouldn't should he break.

Pulling away, she locked eyes with him, grasping his arms so he'd feel her solidity. "I'm here," she stated firmly. "I'm home."

He closed his eyes and nodded, pressing his forehead to hers. Wendy sighed, wishing to stay there a while more, wanting to explain everything. But shock was a dwindling thing, and in a crowd of boys it was soon bound to break. Now wasn't the time to reminisce.

"Come on," she prodded with a smile. "Shouldn't you be crowing?"

His face split into a dimpled grin, eyes brightening by the second. Then head toward the sky, Peter Pan crowed with such enthusiasm and triumph that none but Wendy could ever tell it was only for show, for the Lost Boys. Cheers and shouts erupted with whoops of joy and incredulous laughter all throughout the clearing.

When Peter smiled back down at Wendy, she giggled in her own growing excitement. Then she turned to meet the surge of Lost Boys and they swarmed toward her. Tootles popped up first, throwing his short arms around her waist. After that, everyone was a blur of wrestling each other to see Wendy next. The glow in her chest enhanced with each boy she embraced, each hand she squeezed, each head of hair she ruffled.

They're my family, Wendy felt in warm assurance. *Every last one of them.*

She knew them each by name... except one.

● ● ●

A girl stood on the edge of the clearing, watching from a distance. Black hair fell to her shoulders, thin bangs over dark brown eyes. She didn't look much older than fifteen, and her clothes were a tad too big. There was something about her, something familiar...

"Why is she here?"

Wendy flipped her attention to Peter. "Who?"

He stuck his chin up toward something behind her. "Tiger Lily."

Tiger Lily.

With a sigh, she turned toward the Chieftess who stepped into the clearing as if she'd been called forward, head high and stone faced. The Lost Boys retreated quickly behind Wendy and Peter.

"We have matters to discuss," Tiger Lily said evenly.

"Matters?" Peter questioned. "What matters?"

"I'll explain later," Wendy insisted.

Tiger Lily's eyes hardened. "Our agreement was—"

"I know what our agreement was, and I'll honor it. But right now, I have more pressing things to figure out."

"Of course. Do you have more frivolous reunions to attend to, or is there another trap you wish to leave me stranded in?"

"Don't tempt me."

"Hey," Red cut in, running up to stand between them. "Watch it, princess. Remember where you are."

Tiger Lily glared.

Peter stepped forward, brow knit together. "Who are you?"

Before Wendy could explain, Tiger Lily spoke up, "Wendy's new wolf pet."

Clenching her fists, Red grit her teeth. "Hold your tongue, or else…"

"Else what? You reveal your claws?" Tiger Lily dared. "But you cannot. Neverland holds it back, does it not?"

Wendy caught Red's arm to hold her back, noting how tight her muscles were. "That's enough, Tiger Lily."

"Yes, I think so."

Red socked her in the jaw, breaking out of Wendy's hold. The Lost Boys roared, egging them on. Wendy stood shocked as Tiger Lily wiped the blood from her mouth.

"I don't need claws," Red growled.

Tiger Lily huffed, righting herself again. "Neither do I."

Wendy saw it coming, grabbing Red's arm to pull her back. But Peter darted forward, snatching Tiger Lily's forearm before she could retaliate. Daggers shot from their eyes, each daring the other to make a move. By this time the Lost Boys were getting anxious, waiting to see what would happen. Wendy's heart pounded.

"That's enough," Peter said lowly. "Whatever business you bring will be discussed later."

Tiger Lily scowled, ripping her arm away. But she didn't retaliate. With a stiff neck, she turned and left the clearing. Where she went, Wendy decided not to concern herself with.

When Peter turned back to her with raised eyebrows, she tried not to smile. Before she could try to explain what was going on, Red rubbed her bruised crimson knuckles and grinned. "I'm Red, friend of Wendy's."

"Friend?"

"We met at an insane asylum."

Bells rang in mass chaos through the air before Wendy could clarify Red's statement. Her heart pounded when she heard the voices behind them, the call for Peter.

"Where are you?!" chimed a voice she knew. "There's something—"

Three pixies sped into the clearing, each one coming to a halt at the sight. Wendy smiled, elated.

"Tink!"

The fairy paused, blinked, then zoomed forward so fast that a Lost Boy's hat flew off at her passing. Wendy didn't flinch when Tink stopped just before her nose, face scarlet. "Wendy Moira Angela Darling, don't you ever do that again!" she scolded with such severity it could've been sincere.

"Get kidnapped?"

"Die."

Wendy smiled sadly, deciding not to answer that request. "It's good to see you, Tink."

Tinker Bell made a face, pinching Wendy's nose. "I guess it's good to see you, too."

"Did you find him?!"

Wendy snapped her head around, completely ecstatic when Alice burst out of the jungle.

Coming to a halt, Alice looked around at the many faces now staring at her. "Oh. Well, I suppose that's taken care of."

"Another friend of yours?" Peter questioned.

"Yup. That's Alice."

Alice smiled and waved, awkwardly trying to make her way through the crowd of Lost Boys. Wendy heard some of the boys whispering in confusion. She sighed. There was a lot of explaining to do.

"Alice, you're safe!" Red exclaimed.

"Yeah, I had a slight detour, but it turned out well enough," Alice stated, finally making it to them.

"I guess we did, too," Red admitted, still massaging her fist.

Peter took Wendy's arm and pulled her closer. "What's going on?" he questioned.

"They're friends, you can trust them. They arrived here with me," Wendy explained. "We got separated when Kyta was chasing us."

"How'd you get on Neverpeak without anyone noticing?"

"It's a long story. I can explain—"

The Lost Boys shifted toward the sound of new voices coming from the jungle. Wendy turned with them, but it took a while for her to make out what the voices were saying.

"Trust me, kid, don't let them fool you, bunnies are tricky. And Long Ears may well be the worst of the lot."

Alice raised an eyebrow.

"Man, I never would have thought rabbits could be so horrible," another familiar voice exclaimed.

"Trust me, Nibs, that White Rabbit is on his own level of pompousness."

Jack emerged from the thicket grinning, a skinny boy right behind him. The kid's face brightened. "Wendy!"

"Nibs!" She braced herself before he slammed into her, laughing at his tight hug.

"Jack told me, he *told* me you were alive!" Nibs said excitedly. "I almost didn't believe him."

"Took some convincing and an emotional breakdown to get him to believe I wasn't crazy," Jack admitted, trying to avoid Alice's disapproving look.

Wendy shook her head amusedly. He should really watch it before he started to rant about the White Rabbit.

"Jack, you're alive!" Red stated, unable to mask her relief.

Jack shrugged. "I take it you missed me, Rubes?"

"Rubes?" She cocked her head. "That's new."

"What? You don't like it?"

"No, it's just... that's what my father used to call me."

Wendy noticed the shredded fabric first, pulling away from Nibs with growing concern. "Jack, are you bleeding?"

Eyes dropping sheepishly, he shuffled his feet. "*Maybe.*"

Wendy groaned, coming over to take a look for herself. "Boys..."

"What? It's just a scratch!"

The shirt was ripped from three different angles, and the skin beneath it matched in bloody burgundy. What did Jack get himself into?

Red took one look and scowled. "Just a *scratch*?!"

"What happened?" Wendy questioned.

"Ah, you should've *seen* him!" Nibs exclaimed suddenly, waving his arms around to demonstrate. "Jack fought about *twenty* pirates single handedly! He swung his staff with expert speed, knocking pirate after pirate aside. And then, after all the pirates were taken care of, a giant *cougar* came out of nowhere! Jack battled the beast, even after he was wounded by her vicious claws."

"What do you know, he almost spins as tall a tale as you do, Jack," Alice spoke up.

"Alright, let's get something straight," Jack countered, "what you heard earlier, I wasn't talking about Long Ears."

"Uh huh."

"I mean, what gave you the crazy notion to think I was talking about the White Rabbit? Are you mad? I could've been talking about any white bunny!"

"Sure."

"You don't know how many pompous rabbits I've come across in my life."

"You know, maybe I should've asked for some of those shrinking pastries you *willingly ate* to remind you in moments like these of your lowest point in life."

Jack smirked. "The funny thing is you actually think *that* was the lowest point in my life."

Wendy tried to peal some of the shirt away from the wounds, but Jack flinched and his back began to bleed again. "These need to be washed and stitched."

"I can do that," Red offered. "You need to talk to Pan. We're still missing Kai."

"Oh, is this the famous Peter Pan?" Jack asked, pointing to the Lost Boy's leader. He stuck out his hand. "Hey, I'm Jack."

With a moment's hesitation, Peter shook it. "Another friend from the insane asylum?"

"Insane asylum; is that what she told you? You must think we're mad then! Well, I mean, one of us is..."

Alice made a face at him.

"I meant it in the best way possible," Jack said defensively.

Wendy met Peter's confused gaze, her heart pounding. Before anything else could interrupt her, she went up to him. "I want to explain everything. But first, Red needs supplies to tend to Jack's back. It's been ripped apart. And we need to put Tiger Lily somewhere she won't cause issues."

"I can get Curly to get the supplies, and the Twins can take them someplace for now. As for Tiger Lily..." He frowned. "I don't know what to do with her."

Wendy thought a moment, looking at Alice with the brunette fairy on her shoulder. "We can put her in my room, with Alice and the fairies. That way she's out of the way, and Alice can keep her under control."

"That could work... except..."

"What?"

"There's something you should know—Jane!"

Confused, Wendy turned around to find the girl she'd seen earlier coming their way. *Jane. Where did she come from? Why was she so familiar?*

Jane smiled. "So you're Wendy. I've heard a lot about you."

"You have?"

"Well, you can wrestle anything out of Slightly with enough persuasion."

Wendy couldn't help but smile. She knew that much was true.

"Jane is the newest member of the gang," Peter explained. "She came in on a Lost Boat a while back, and she's proved herself to be quite the Lost Girl."

"It's nice to meet you, then, Jane," Wendy said, managing a smile

"And you," Jane returned. "Welcome home."

Shadows lengthened and the wind turned cool. The day was wearing thin and there was still much to be done. After sending Curly off to grab the medical supplies, the Twins came forward to lead Jack and Red away.

"We'll see you all later," Red said as they started off.

"If I don't die from whatever torture you call *healing*," Jack grumbled as she dragged him off.

In passing Jane, Wendy noticed Red pause to examine her, saw them lock eyes for but a moment before Red moved on her way again. Unsure what she'd just witnessed, Wendy turned back to those remaining.

"Jane, could you take Alice and Tiger Lily back to Wendy's room?" Peter asked. "And Tink, you and your friends are free to stay as always."

Jane raised an eyebrow, but nodded, beckoning Alice to follow. The fairies flew after them, after Tink took a moment to fly around Wendy and Peter happily. As the Lost Boys had long dispersed, the clearing was left considerably empty.

Peter turned back to her. "After you."

● ● ●

CHAPTER FOURTEEN
MEMORIES

"Hold still," Red ordered, allowing it to come as a bark.

Jack met the cold touch of her wet rag with a flinch, which didn't help with the bleeding. She noticed the tension in his jaw as he buried his face in the pillow; holding back a cry or complaint, she couldn't tell. Though she knew the pain bit more than he was letting on, Red diligently cleaned his wounds. Slashes split his back like crimson barbed wire.

"You're killing me, Rubes," Jack groaned into his pillow.

"Healing, remember," she corrected, "the worst kind of torture."

The grin came first before he turned his head to look up at her. She ignored his stare. Scrubbing the dried blood too roughly earned another grimace and hiss of pain from him. His back muscles tightened. Fresh blood dribbled out again. Setting her jaw, Red tried to be more tender with his bare back.

"Did you really save that boy?" she asked.

Jack smirked. "Didn't you hear Nibs? He told the whole story."

"I'm not so sure that was the whole story."

"Fair enough. Maybe it wasn't *twenty* pirates, and I didn't exactly come in swinging. It was more like two pirates that I managed to sneak up on and gave them a knock on the head with an oversized stick. Don't tell the others, though."

She just chuckled in response. Setting aside the stained rag, she began laying bandages on his back. Curly

• • •

had mentioned something about their being coated in some sort of homemade medical cream. They were certainly slick to the touch.

"You've never talked about your family before."

Her stomach tightened. What had led up to that statement?

"You said your dad used to call you Rubes," Jack hinted. "So far, that's the only thing I know about you *before* the Enchanted Forest. Even your time *in* the Enchanted Forest I don't know much about."

Red hesitated, trying to ignore the swelling in her throat. "My family, my life before all of this, was... complicated."

"How so?" Jack asked, cringing as she laid another bandage on his wounds.

"I don't like to talk about it. I'm not proud of the kind of business my family and I were part of," Red admitted, leaving out that she wasn't proud of many things she'd done. "I've tried to keep the past behind me."

"What happened to them?"

She waited until she felt she could speak without choking up. "My parents died when I was thirteen. I lived with my grandmother for a long time, but I couldn't get out of the business my family had been in."

"What was this bad business?" Jack asked. She was very aware of the look he gave her, that terrible concern. "You can tell me."

Red let herself meet his gaze, stirred by his sincerity.

I know, she thought, *but right now I just can't.*

But all she said was, "Maybe someday."

He studied her a moment more. "Alright."

• • •

Relaxing some, she turned back to her task. "Fang started following me about a year after my parents died, observing from a distance. I managed to shake him off my trail a couple times, staying in public places, out in the open. But one day when I was taking a shortcut through the woods to my grandmother's, the one place I've ever been safe, Fang caught up. I hid in a hollow tree and found myself in the Enchanted Forest."

His brow furrowed. "How long did you stay there?"

"Three years."

"Three years!"

"Lay still!" Red scolded when he nearly jumped up. "If you reopen your wounds again, I will hit you."

Jack eyed her bruising knuckles, probably realizing she wasn't joking. He settled down but still gaped. "*Three years?* I thought it was just a few months, maybe a year."

She shook her head.

"What all *happened*?"

"I don't want to talk about it," she said before the memories could emerge. "Let's just say my story involves a lot more than that of *Little Red Riding Hood*."

He made a face. "You just love to be a mystery, don't you, Rubes?"

Yes, she thought but didn't dare admit. *It's safer that way.*

With a groan, Jack vowed, "Fine, don't tell me. But one day I'll figure you out, Rubina Ellen Daim. I can promise you that!"

She paused, looking at him curiously. Why? Why would he care? Why should he try to expose her? It almost scared her to think that he just might succeed.

• • •

Brushing it off, she sat back in her chair. "I'll have to change the bandages later. Then we'll see if there's enough skin to stitch you up."

"Of course," Jack groaned, situating himself into a more comfortable position on the cot. "The worst is always yet to come."

Red huffed. But he just smiled, closing his eyes. She watched him, her mind wandering. What if he did find out, they all found out, about her past, about the person she tried to bury? She tried to hide it, but every day she could feel herself leaking back out of the shadows. Rubbing her bruised knuckles, she realized how easy it was to relapse into it, the impulsion, the anger, the incapability to justify her actions... the indifference on whether her actions were justified.

But she did care. She cared now. What would happen if they ever found out? What would they think of her? Would they see her past, see her exposed, and abandon her? But what if they understood?

It doesn't matter if they would understand. It's not worth the risk. I can't be abandoned again.

Cocking her head, Red voiced, "What about you?"

His eyes popped open. "What about me?"

"While we're on the subject of pasts, what about yours? You don't talk much about it much either, you know."

"What are you talking about? I'm an open book!"

She almost laughed humorlessly. In her experience, no one was ever an open book. Everyone had secrets. It's simply how many secrets you kept that determined trustworthiness and openness. By the way he was steadily looking at her, Red could only guess he was contemplating how many of his secrets he should share.

• • •

Jack's voice was soft when he broke the silence. "My parents were killed in a cattle stampede."

Her abdomen clenched. "I'm sorry, I didn't…"

"Don't be." He shrugged it off. "It happened a long time ago. Besides, the orphanage wasn't so bad."

There was a gleam in his eyes she could not decipher. Was it longing? Nostalgia? Either way, those were feelings she was afraid she no longer possessed.

Jack grinned, his look distant. "I guess you could say I had my own band of lost boys and girls. That's where I met Harry and Jill. We grew up together, best friends all our lives. We'd lead the other kids on adventures and expeditions…" He paused, a sadness creeping into his voice, "We never realized the three of us would end up going on a real one ourselves."

"And the orphanage?"

"As far as I know, it's still where it's always been. Someday, I hope to go back and pay my old pals a visit."

Go back?

Could she even imagine it? All this time, Red had been running away from all she'd left behind, especially back in Europe. But did that have to mean leaving every*one* behind? Her grandmother… was she still waiting for her? Would she even recognize her now, after everything that's happened? It had been nearly five years since Red had seen her grandmother. But maybe she would visit her after all of this was over, as Jack said about his returning to the orphanage. Maybe she would never see her at all…

"Blast it! I almost forgot," Jack's exclamation jolted her back to reality, "would you mind…?"

He extended his hand, palm up to reveal the sprinkle of splinters in his skin too tiny to see clearly. Biting back a smile, she took his hand and began working at picking the splinters out with her nails. His fingers curled in pain.

"Do I even want to know?" Red laughed.

"Blackberries."

She decided not to tell him these were more like stinging nettle than blackberry thorns. The blackberries would've been easier to get out.

After a moment of silence, Jack cleared his throat. "What do you think of… whatever her name is?"

"Tiger Lily?" Red guessed with a growl.

"Who's Tiger Lily?"

"… Just some princess who doesn't know when to keep her mouth shut."

Thankfully, he didn't press, but she could tell he noticed her bruising knuckles.

"Well, that's not who I was *intending*," Jack admitted. "I meant the other one, the Lost Girl or whatever."

Her throat tightened. It didn't take long to confess, "I don't trust her."

He frowned. "Why?"

Because she reminds me of myself.

She knew it from the look in the girl's eyes, the secrets and shadows, the mask she wore so carefully. But she didn't dare admit that.

Red shook her head. "She's hiding something; I can feel it. Something about her isn't right."

"You haven't really given her a chance. She might not be as bad as you think."

"How do you know?"

● ● ●

"I don't." Jack's gaze drifted, distant. "But don't we all deserve a chance before we're judged?"

Her brow furrowed curiously. Was he talking about himself elusively? Maybe she couldn't read him as well as she'd thought. Maybe he really did have chapters he kept hidden despite his insistence of openness.

Focusing intently on his splintered palm, she lied, "I suppose so."

*****

Walking through the jungles of Neverland with Peter by her side, everything seemed right again. Grass met their feet in a cushion. The breeze swirled around them. Nocturnal creatures woke early just to greet them with wide eyes, as if they'd been waiting for this reunion and respected its solace enough not to disturb.

Long out of earshot without a chance of being discovered, Peter stopped. Wendy turned to him, finding his arms trembling and teeth grinding as if he was trying so hard to keep it together, so hard to stop himself from breaking.

"Peter," she spoke gently, touching his arm. "It's alright."

"No, it's not," he spoke at last, voice strained through grit teeth. His face grew red and blotchy. Glassy eyes looked anywhere but at her. "You were dead. You were gone."

A lump formed in her throat. "I know."

He breathed deeply, shakily. "I couldn't save you; couldn't find you." The anger in his voice grew painfully. "I should've stopped them."

"Peter, don't—"

"It shouldn't have happened. I should've heard them coming. I shouldn't have let them get to you." The words came in a rush with every anxious exhale as if he were bleeding them, cutting them out of his heart. "They hurt you, took you; I should've seen it coming! I should've *stopped* them!"

"Peter, look at me," Wendy ordered, grabbing him by the shoulders, forcing him to look her in the eye. "Look at me!"

He obeyed, bloodshot eyes finally meeting hers. She had seen this side of Peter before, the broken bit, the part of him he hid from the world even as it drove everything he did in life. But even so, she had never seen him so close to shattering. Not even when he'd woken at night screaming from what he'd seen in his sleep. In a place where dreams come true, nightmares are the most terrible. And this was worse. This was much worse.

Taking a deep breath, Wendy stated strongly, "You can't change the past. Don't do this to yourself!"

He swallowed hard as if every word in his throat were a bristling bramble. Voice raw, his words came in scarred edges, "I lost you."

"I'm right here, Peter!" she pressed, taking his hands, grasping them firmly. "I'm right here."

Squeezing his eyes shut, he bowed his head and brought her hands in his to his brow, choking on sobs. Then he crumbled. All strength left him as he fell to his knees crying, clutching her hands still. Wendy knelt down with him, tears sliding down her own cheeks. Knees touching his, leaning close, she willed him to feel her presence.

You're not alone, Peter. You'll never lose me.

But words couldn't be spoken, not now. They had to be felt. So she cried with him and for him all at once, the kind of thing you only do for those you love.

When Peter's breathing came heavily steady, Wendy looked up. He still had his head bowed, but the crying had done him some good it seemed. She pressed a kiss to his knuckles, which brought his gaze up to hers. An encouraging half smile tugged the corner of her mouth. He met it with one as if to say thanks. It was enough.

With a deep breath, Peter released her hands and fell back to lay in the grass, staring at the stars. Wendy crawled over to lay beside him.

"Where did you go?" he asked, his voice losing its graininess.

"Home," she responded. "London that is."

"But, we looked there and couldn't find you, only your parents. We even searched your brothers' place. We searched the whole city, the whole country; everywhere and anywhere you could possibly be."

"I didn't stay long. A psychiatric facility took me away, locked me underground for over a year. That's where I met Red, Jack, Kai, and Alice."

"Your friends are psychotic?"

She laughed, "No more than I am!"

"That's not reassuring."

She elbowed him, but he just smiled.

There's the Peter Pan I know and love.

"We were each in the Facility because we've known magic, or traveled to another world," she explained. "They called us psychotic, though. But someone helped us escape."

"Who?"

She shrugged. "A woman; called herself Anne Christiansen. After that, we ended up in a place called Wonderland."

"*Wonderland?*" he asked, sounding astonished and confused.

She turned to look at him. "You know of it?"

Peter nodded, the moons' pale light illuminating his face. "I've heard of it; never been there, though. A bandersnatch found its way here once. That's not an adventure I'd go looking for again."

Wendy nodded, recalling the nasty beasts. The stars swirled above, blinking in golds, reds, and silvers. She felt the brush of Peter's hand over her knuckles, smiled when he wove his fingers through hers. He might not have been better, but she knew he would be.

Don't go. Don't take this away.

She wasn't sure why she thought it or who she was thinking it to. But with everything they've faced and everything they had yet to face, she wished nothing more.

Yet there were things that couldn't be ignored, no matter how much it threatened her wishes.

"I need to tell you something," she said softly; Peter tilting his head to listen. "Do you remember the first time we met?" She explained the White Rabbit's theory of how someone may have been responsible for his Shadow coming to her window, explained the mysterious master of the Queen of Hearts and how, for some reason, they wanted Wendy and her friends. Peter's brow furrowed as her story progressed.

"Have you," she started, "heard anything about some power rising, threatening the realms, growing its forces?"

He shook his head. "This is a first. I haven't left the Island much since you've been gone, and as far as I know…" His frown deepened. "I'm actually not sure what Hook has been up to. He hasn't been seen; pretty smart of him. And since my Shadow…"

His voice trailed off. The air stilled and Wendy could hear the animals scurry away anxiously.

Worried, she asked, "You alright?"

"Yeah, I just realized…" He shook his head. "Never mind. I think Tink may know something; she's been traveling a lot."

"I'll ask her about it. Just one more thing."

"Yes?"

"Kai," she explained, "a friend of mine, he's missing somewhere here. Do you think you and the boys could find him?"

Sitting up, Peter rubbed the back of his neck uncertainly. "You know that this isn't the best place to get lost in. There are places even I haven't explored, or don't remember—"

"Kai's a survivor," Wendy insisted. "If anyone can handle Neverland alone, it's him."

The look he gave her was terribly concerned—he honestly didn't have to worry about her so much—but he relented. "We'll keep a look out for him. But… don't get your hopes up."

She grinned. "Get my hopes up? That doesn't sound like me at all."

*****

"Make yourselves at home," Jane welcomed, leading the strange group into the treehouse.

● ● ●

143

Poking her head out of the floor, Alice looked around the spacious room. Two walls yawned into windows draped with mismatched curtains. The third held a thick fur covering the doorway; and the back wall wrapped around the bared tree trunk dotted with fairy houses. She could imagine Wendy living here, arranging new trinkets and treasures on the shelves as the Lost Boys gave them to her. A simple wooden bird sat on the untouched bed.

"You sleep on the floor?" spoke Tiger Lily as she emerged from the trapdoor.

Alice noticed the sleeping mat and blanket laying in the middle of the floor, the very thing the Chieftess raised her eyebrow at. Jane looked at it too, as if just realizing its presence for the first time.

"Yeah," she admitted sheepishly, "it didn't feel right disturbing a room that wasn't *meant* for me."

"Ah, ghosts," Tiger Lily acknowledged grimly.

Jane shrugged. "Just a suspicion."

Tink suddenly flew in through the window, Hazel and Sparrow following close behind. The three pixies sat on a nearby shelf, Sparrow nearly tripping over a glass marble.

"Alice, right?" Jane started, sitting on her sleeping mat cross-legged. "Where are you from?"

Alice perched herself on the bed's edge. "I lived with my father in Daresbury, England. I wouldn't call it my home, though."

"Was your father killed?"

Tiger Lily huffed, folding her arms and leaning against the wall. "If one's father dies, that does not have to mean you no longer have a home."

"I wasn't saying that," Jane replied, unfazed. "I didn't exactly *assume*. I only, I don't know, *wondered*."

Alice interjected before this could escalate, "No, my father isn't dead. It's just... I realized that it wasn't home to me anymore."

"Where is it then?" Jane inquired, "Home?"

She sighed, thoughts of her Mad Hatter flicking through her mind. "A place called Wonderland."

Maybe she expected a question about it, what it was, where it was. But Jane didn't seem to pay it much thought. She just kind of bobbed her head as if she understood or was pretending to, then turned to Tiger Lily. "And then you're the Chieftess, huh? How's that working out for you?"

Back stiffening, she looked out the window. "Fine."

"Is it hard having to take charge without your parents there?"

Tiger Lily narrowed her eyes. "What is this, some kind of twisted interrogation?"

"No." Jane shrugged. "I'm just genuinely curious."

"Well you are breaching the boundaries of appropriate inquiry."

"Sorry; didn't mean to pry or offend. It's been a while since I've spoken to other... girls."

Tiger Lily just scowled. She seemed very good at that.

Before the silence could get any more awkward, Alice asked, "What about you, Jane? Where are you from?"

"I wandered the Mainland before I came here on a Lost Boat."

"Didn't you have a mother?" Hazel piped up in a rattle of bells from her seat atop a shelf.

Sparrow nudged her. "If she did, then wouldn't she still be there on the Mainland?"

The fairy blanched. "Ah, jingles. I didn't think…"

Jane wrenched her head around in confusion. "What're they saying?"

Tiger Lily gave the shortest shrug. Strange, seeing as Alice had assumed that she could understand the pixies as well.

"Hazel was just asking about your mother," she interpreted.

Jane frowned, as if reaching into the dustiest corners of her memory where all was a struggle to pull out again. "I… I don't remember my mother. She's dead, I think."

Alice lowered her eyes empathetically. "My mother's dead, too."

An empty pit formed in her chest. She knew what it was like to grow up without ever knowing a mother, to miss someone she had never known. Apparently she looked just like her, though. It was the reason why her father couldn't look at her for long, would never meet her eyes. Alice had always hated that she looked like her mother.

"And your father?" Tiger Lily asked evenly.

Jane looked away. "I don't like to talk about him."

CHAPTER FIFTEEN
SKULL ROCK

Kai had tried to avoid it for as long as possible, gathering driftwood, catching fish, but he could prolong it no longer. The tide was coming in quickly, and Sylvia was waiting.

Limping after her, Kai eyed the looming Skull Rock that only seemed to grow as they approached. Its grotesquely wrenched open mouth waited to swallow him whole. The air turned bitter. Slimy water slid down the barnacled rock's sides. An aroma of sea salt and fish hit his senses in a sour blow.

Even with the slight glow of Sylvia's aura, Kai couldn't see hardly anything at first. The darkness was shifting and light was reflective off the wetness of the walls. Then he blinked and it was like the shadows took on form, then murky light. He tried to swallow the knot in his throat.

Ghosts.

Some flitted by in mere wisps of distinction, others had such a realistic materiality about them he almost thought them alive. As his eyes adjusted to the cave's darkness, they also adjusted to the visual existence of the ghosts. He flinched away from a kid that ran past him, one he mistakenly took to be real until the kid *floated* up to snatch the hat off of an unsuspecting pirate.

Holding his bundle of wood and the two fish he'd caught close to him, Kai did the best he could to avoid touching these spirits. Pressure built behind his ears as if it was ready to let loose another stream of pain and memories that were not his own. But the ghosts drifted out of Sylvia

● ● ●

and his way, either staring at him with curiosity or ignoring him in disinterest. Then the dog came, small and scrappy, and darted straight through his leg. The ice cut through his shin, willing him to crumple...

The smell of smoke and blood filling his lungs.

Teeth gleaming in the firelight, and a breath so foul he wanted to choke instead of scream.

When the spots retreated from his vision, Kai found Sylvia looking back at him with concern. He nodded it off, continuing after her.

A wiry old man huddled up against the wall caught his attention. The ghost's eyes were wide, so wide Kai wondered if he was missing his eyelids. Knotted hands clutched knobby knees, his breathing wet like he was drowning. But he trembled uncontrollably, with moans that came out in pitiful huffs and spasms. A young girl sat near him, unsuccessfully trying to comfort the man.

"What's the matter with him?" Kai asked his escort.

"Some of us handle the pain worse than others."

"Pain?"

"Aye, pain. It is our curse."

The cave's back sloped up into a loop that led straight to one of the skull's eyes. It was drier there, no other ghosts besides Sylvia. And it was warm, the sun's dying rays shining through the opening. He could see the Island clearly from here, a jungle that waited for him just across the channel.

"Stay here until the morning," Sylvia spoke. "The tide will flood the mouth below, making it deadly to the living. Do not come down, even when..." But she hesitated.

• • •

148

"Even when what?" Kai pressed, not keen on surprises.

"Even when you hear the screams." She was completely stone faced, an expression that should not accompany such a statement.

Setting down his load and preparing a fire, Kai tried not to let it bother him. But Sylvia just stood there, her presence seeming to impress upon him that she was not telling him something. And those images... they haunted him in a way they shouldn't.

As flames arose from his labors, Kai felt a chill go up his spine right before the gruff voice of Long John spoke, "You head on down. I'll stay here with him 'til nightfall."

Looking over his shoulder, Kai saw Sylvia nod appreciatively, giving him one last look before disappearing down the slope. Long John stood there alone. His muscles clenched, ready to jump out of the way should the ghost decide to attack him again. When no such thing happened, he continued preparing his fish, keeping the ghost in his sights at all times.

By the time he had his meal flayed and poised over the fire, Long John was standing so close either one of them could touch the other if they reached out. Thankfully, Kai noted, he was leaning so heavily on his crutch that there would be some warning movement should he try anything, enough for Kai to dive out of the way.

"You survived a mermaid attack, eh?"

Long John wasn't looking at him, but Kai gave a cautious nod.

"Lucky, that. Only a handful live to tell such a tale," Long John stated, his gaze on the firelight. "It's the most beautiful death you'll ever know."

"Why are you here?" Kai questioned suspiciously.

"I'm cursed here, lad."

"You weren't so civil earlier."

"And you think that's changed?"

Kai's shoulders tensed, his grip tightening on the stick he was using to turn the fish. Unfortunately, he knew that was useless. No weapon could save him from this demon. Long John knew it too, taking one look at his clenched fist and giving a huff.

"I promised Sylvia I'd give you a chance," he muttered.

"A chance at what?"

"To prove I shouldn't kill you. Don't squander it so quickly."

Kai grit his teeth. "You can't kill me."

"What makes you say that?"

"You'd be ripped apart."

Kai stared levelly at him, trying not to reveal his bluff. As far as he knew, *whatever* it was about him that hurt the ghosts may not actually kill them. But he also figured that neither Long John nor Sylvia knew the extent of pain they'd undergo should they step through him again.

Long John didn't bat an eye. "After barely existing for so long in this hell, you think I wouldn't welcome it?"

Kai had no response. *What's he going to do?*

He turned away, sat down with a groan and stared at the fire. "Stop wasting your time. I know what you're doing. You're analyzing, figuring out what to expect, how you can best benefit. But it won't work, not with us. Unlike the living, we've got nothing to lose. You can't predict what ghosts will do."

"But you can guess."

"Yes, but what real good does that do?"

Stoking the fire, Kai pulled out the browned fish and let it cool on a rock. Finally, he decided to be blunt. "What do you want from me? Why am I here?"

"Neverbird brought you. I know you didn't forget that one."

"Is it that simple?"

"Yeah, sometimes things are that simple."

"Then what do you want from me?"

He sighed, looked away towards the setting sun. "Sylvia thinks you can save us."

Kai scowled. Those words again... he couldn't seem to escape them. Why did everyone think he could save them? He couldn't even save the one person who mattered most.

Scratching his scar, he thought, *I've never even been able to save myself.*

"We're all cursed, every one of us," Long John went on, "even Skippy."

Kai raised an eyebrow.

"The dog."

He grunted acknowledgement, but didn't pursue the matter.

Long John stared at him. "You're not even curious what the curse is? Why we're cursed? How some sick fiend went as far as to curse a bloody dog?"

Kai shrugged. The more he knew about this curse, the more these ghosts would expect him to rescue them from it.

• • •

What's more, he was afraid that the more he knew about it, then the more he would actually *care*.

How many times will this happen? Someone thinks I can save them, and when I try to, I fail them.

But Long John smiled slightly at his mask of indifference. "I'm starting to like you, lad. You remind me of myself."

"And that's supposed to make me feel better?"

"No." He paused, looked away again. "Still not going to ask what happened to us?"

"*Nej.*"

"I'm gonna tell you anyway."

He'd figured as much.

"Long time ago, before the feud, some pirates were made aware that the variety of beasts on the Island could be used to make profit on the Mainland. Over hunting grew, things got out of hand. The Panther Tribe weren't too happy about it, especially when certain hunters only harvested certain parts. They started raiding bands of pirates that ventured too far into the jungle. But things only escalated, and soon it was getting hard to find food lest you wanted to risk wiping out the beasts. No amount of portals could refurbish it without time." Long John huffed. "Time. Isn't it funny? This place is timeless, yet it still depends on it."

"What does this have to do with anything?"

"Backstory. Only way to explain anything without many questions. Now, no more interruptions or I'll show it rather than tell it."

Kai clenched his jaw, deciding not to test him.

"Anyway, because the pirates had plenty of food, the Lost Boys took to stealing some a little at a time. No use in letting anything go to waste, that's what they thought. But rumors spread quickly when people started noticing things missing, or caught glimpses of small shadows in the night. Then one of them was caught, and when Pan came back for him, he saw the kid shot and Hook held the smoking gun." He pinched the bridge of his nose, squeezing his eyes like he could see it. When he recovered, he continued, "Didn't take long before the Lost Boys attacked. It was a bloody battle, the kind that shouldn't have been as terrible as it was. I wasn't even supposed to be there, happened on this island while trying to reach... never mind, that's not important. Anyway, next thing I knew, there was an explosion. Blew me to bits; died instantly. The bomb was an accident, but it was Pan who caused it. He and Hook fought in an epic duel, fire blazing all around, smoke billowing in mushrooms."

Kai didn't bother to ask how he knew what this *epic duel* looked like if he'd already died by then.

"Hook lost his hand that night, that bloody ticking crocodile eating it right in front of him. Shortly after that, the Lost Boys retreated. There's been the feud between them ever since." Long John scowled. "An old and powerful tribesman watched the battle, cursed all who died that night to this bloody existence. Don't know what the blasted fool was thinking. Only a powerful magic can release us. That's where you come in."

"Because you think I can save you."

"Because we think you know someone who can save us."

Kai instinctively touched his scar. He couldn't deny it; he'd said it himself. It wasn't just the Snow Queen either. There were many powers that lay in that cursed realm, each a force to be reckoned with. But the chill of the Snow Queen's presence was seeping into the shadows of his memory.

Long John nodded. "Whatever that thing on your face is, it's powerful stuff. So powerful we ghosts can *feel* it. If you know of someone who can harness it, then you know who can release us."

He stared at the fire, trying not to look at the ghost. It was all silent for a long time, but it was the kind of waiting silence that Kai knew meant Long John wasn't finished yet. Beginning to eat his meal, he tried to ignore the burnt scales and bitter taste.

"I was never supposed to be here," Long John said softly, looking around at the damp stone walls. "I was on a ship ready to start a new life, an honest one. I was going to do something that would make him proud."

"Jim?" Kai guessed, recalling the name from before.

He couldn't tell if the ghost was going to ram through him again or not. But he just nodded solemnly. "Yeah," he huffed a halfhearted laugh. "I've done some bad things in my life, terrible things that haunt me every time I close my eyes. Jim, he was a good kid, nay, a great one. He considered me a friend, a father figure if you can believe it. But I betrayed him. And when he had the chance to put me behind bars where I belonged, he let me leave. Funny how that proved more effective than sentencing me to prison." He sighed, sat a little straighter. "I was going to make him proud of the man I would become. I was finally going to chart my own course, rattle the stars, and then… Then I would deserve it."

"Deserve what?"

"The way he used to look at me, like I was a hero, or something close to one."

●　●　●

Something howled below, and the slosh of water washing against stone. Kai cringed, thinking about the tide rushing into the cave's mouth. The sun had disappeared behind the mountain peaks, but the colors still ran amber along the horizon.

Swallowing another sour bite of fish, Kai questioned, "What's Sylvia's story?"

"Are you certain you want to hear that one?" Long John asked lowly. "It's probably the worst of us all."

"Why?"

"Hers lives on."

His brow furrowed. "Don't all stories live on? Yours?"

"There's a difference between being remembered, lad, and having your absence cause continuous damage to multitudes." Long John passed a hand over his face, light shining through the parrot tattoo on his forearm. "Sylvia was supposed to stay inside with her children, but when the fighting commenced, she wanted to go out and save who she could. Then the explosion happened. An iron ship's hook got her right in the stomach; her death slow and beyond painful. She's the reason James Hook is the man he is today... Revenge is consuming."

Kai scowled, thinking of what that wretched man had done to Wendy. But what did Sylvia have to do with the vengeful pirate? And if her death was the reason why Hook became the villain he is... was she to blame for all the things this feud wrought?

No, she's not responsible, he decided. *But does she think the same way?*

"Well," the ghost stood suddenly, "now you know; now you care. Now you get to decide what you're gonna do next."

Then he turned to drift away.

Kai whipped around to face him. "Where are you going?"

Long John paused, nodded to the greying sky. "Sun's almost gone. Trust me, you don't want to be near a ghost when night falls and the pain kicks in." He turned to leave again, but hesitated. "Tell me something, lad."

Kai waited.

The ghost stared at the fire. "What does it feel?"

"Warm."

"No, not *how*; *what* does it feel?"

He frowned, looking at the flames himself. *What does it feel?* "It throbs, between singeing the hairs off my arms and breathing over my skin."

Long John almost smiled. "Warm…"

Before he could turn away again, Kai spoke up, "Wait! Why did Sylvia's death turn Hook into…?"

"A monster?"

Kai nodded.

Long John's jaw tensed and he looked at the sky just as the night swallowed the sun. Kai thought he was too late. Then the pirate looked right at him, the veins in his throat throbbing with effort. "She was his wife."

*****

"Wendy?"

She turned around to find Jane standing on the rope bridge just outside the treehouse. "Did I wake you?" Wendy questioned in concern.

• • •

Jane shook her head. "No; couldn't sleep."

"Me neither."

She noticed Jane shift uncomfortably and almost smiled. She'd never considered herself very intimidating, at least not when she wasn't intending to be.

"You want to sit?" Wendy offered.

Jane hesitated but obliged, sitting cross legged beside her. Wendy let her legs dangle over the edge. Letting the night play its melody over her, she tried to send the worries and pressures in her mind to rest for the time being. Those things could be dealt with later.

"How long have you loved him," Jane spoke at last, "Peter Pan? When did you figure it out?"

Giving her a look, Wendy wondered what prompted such a question. Was this girl falling for one of her Lost Boys? Which one?

Better not scare her off by asking directly.

She thought back to when a cocky boy flew threw her window for the first time searching for his Shadow, when she'd given that boy a thimble so he wouldn't forget her and called it a kiss. Her hand twisted the acorn hanging around her neck; her happy thought back near her heart where it belonged. A smile tugged the corner of her mouth. "I suppose I've always known, since I was a little girl. I don't think I recognized it at first," she admitted. "Loving him is the most natural thing in the world."

Jane lowered her eyes.

Wendy sighed, breathing in the wind. "I love it out here. This place, this feeling, this time."

"Time…" Jane echoed softly.

● ● ●

"When everyone is asleep at the end of a long day, safe, peaceful. They're rare moments. It's good to enjoy them while they last." She looked up at the stars, how they winked down at her, speaking a language she couldn't understand. "They never last long."

"It seems safe enough here, at least as long as I've been here."

"It's an illusion. Step out of these borders and who knows what you'll find," Wendy explained. "Neverland keeps primary dangers out of Hangman's Tree, making it a haven of sorts."

"Like pirates?"

"Exactly."

"Then how…?"

When Jane didn't finish, Wendy turned to look at her. "What?"

"It's just," Jane blew her bangs out of her eyes, "if that's true, then how were the pirates able to, you know, kidnap you?"

She frowned, a chill running through her. No answer came to her. But Wendy couldn't help but think of something the White Queen, Celeste had said back in Wonderland: *Someone was looking for you, hunting you. They probably still are.*

CHAPTER SIXTEEN
THE STORY OF A BROKEN MAN

"You want to make an allegiance with me?" Peter questioned, raising his eyebrows.

"*Temporary* allegiance," Tiger Lily corrected, stone faced. Wendy could tell she wasn't keen to the position she was in.

"That goes without saying," Curly huffed, crossing his brown arms. "Aren't all of our allegiances temporary?"

Tiger Lily shot him a glare. Though he gulped, he didn't flinch. Wendy suppressed a smile.

"What would this allegiance require?" Peter questioned, caution behind his indifferent exterior. "A raid? Hunting party? We took care of that tiger already."

"Not a beast, Pan," Tiger Lily growled. "Why would I come to such lengths for a beast?"

The Twins seemed to grin in unison, an eerie thing but Wendy knew they were just itching for an adventure. "Pirates."

"Darn it," Slightly muttered, catching Wendy's attention.

"What is it?" she whispered.

He looked at her sheepishly, mouthing, *I forgot...*

But Peter's response to Tiger Lily cut him short. "You want a raid, then? A prank?"

• • •

159

"I do not have time for games. My people have been persecuted for too long by the pirates, and the repercussions of your feud are beyond count, beyond memory."

Peter's face fell, all playfulness spent. "You don't know what you're asking."

"My scouts have informed me that the pirates are gathering, setting anchor in Cannibal Cove unlike anything we've ever seen before. More come in every day," Tiger Lily persisted.

"Uh, Peter."

He turned to Slightly, who grinned awkwardly. Tiger Lily frowned at the interruption, but Peter waited expectantly.

"I kind of forgot to mention earlier," Slightly started, "and it's probably a little late, but..."

"Is this relevant?" Tiger Lily interrupted with a tone that made Wendy grit her teeth.

"Sort of," he confessed. "My teams and I have noticed the same thing she's saying. Ships are leaving Neverland's borders. Pirates are overcrowding Blind Man's Bluff."

"Why didn't you tell us this sooner?" Wendy asked curiously, reading the same question on Peter's face.

Slightly shrugged. "Didn't seem too important until I got news this morning that the *Jolly Roger* has been spotted at Peg Leg Point sailing right into Cannibal Cove. They may be just docking for supplies, but with the swarm of ships already there..."

"The pirates have not gathered like this since before the feud," Tiger Lily cut in, seeming to brighten at Slightly's affirmation. "My father spoke of such a time when he was a child."

"So you're wanting what?" Peter questioned, folding his arms. "To wipe them out?"

"To drive them out."

Peter sighed. "They live here. You can't expect them to leave without a fight."

"My people have lived here longer."

"And mine have lived here longest!"

"Peter," Wendy said softly, trying to cool his rising temper. She met his gaze, watched him take a breath. *Calm down, it's not worth it.*

Tiger Lily paused too, but she was a barricade that couldn't be broken. There was no telling what was going on inside.

The floorboards squeaked under Tootles' feet as he rocked back and forth on his heels in the corner.

"You act as if I beg for a massacre," Tiger Lily spoke at last. "If we join forces, we have a chance at ending the Hook."

Peter burst out a humorless laugh, wagging his finger like he had finally figure it all out. "So that's what this is about: revenge."

"This is not about revenge."

"It's always about revenge! Gosh, everything to do with this feud is about revenge."

"This is about *justice*!"

"Justice? Are you willing to stake your life on that? The lives of your people?" He scowled. "You're asking for war."

"WE ARE ALREADY AT WAR!" Tiger Lily cried, fists clenched at her sides.

Wendy flinched. She hadn't seen the Chieftess lose her temper like this in a long time. Even Peter stepped away slightly at the outburst, but his rising frustration seemed to beg to respond in equal fire.

Hold your tongue, she silently begged of him. *Don't say anything until she's done. Otherwise, this will only escalate.*

"It is no longer a matter of if there is a war; it is a matter of who will strike next." Tiger Lily persisted passionately, "A battle is on our heels, coming upon us. You cannot wait for it to pass you by. It will catch you and you will be wiped out."

Wendy furrowed her brow, the words itching themselves into her head. *What does she know about a war, a battle?*

She had always been aware of the insight Tiger Lily seemed to have, but she'd always assumes it had something to do with being able to read people. This was different.

Does Tiger Lily know about this Master we're supposed to find?

Peter worked his jaw in frustration. Tiger Lily waited, but he didn't respond.

She exclaimed in anger, "You are an IMBECILE, Pan!"

"YOU DON'T THINK I WANT HIM DEAD?!" Peter yelled, the veins in his neck bulging. "AFTER EVERYTHING HE'S DONE! EVERYTHING HE'S FORCED ME TO BECOME!"

• • •

He was so close to Tiger Lily he could have spat on her, but she stood rigid. "Then why do you do nothing?"

Peter breathed heavily, lowering his tone to a growl, "I have more than just myself to look out for."

"What if we don't have to fight?" came a voice beside them.

Wendy looked at Nibs who stood straighter under everyone's gaze.

Don't fight? she thought, ideas churning.

Tiger Lily scowled, annoyed at the intervention. "What then do you suggest? Diplomacy?"

Wringing his hands, Nibs muttered, "Well, I didn't exactly think that far, but when you put it like that..."

"No, Nibs is on the right track," Wendy spoke up, mind racing as things started coming together. "What if we don't have to fight? Or at least, not right away. We could set up a team to observe what's going on at Blind Man's Bluff, find out why the pirates are gathering. If it's really so crowded, no one will notice a few more faces amongst them."

"If they find reason to attack," Slightly added, smile twitching, "they'll inform troops standing by and we'll strike. If not—"

"We go home," one Twin piped up.

"As if nothing had happened," the other followed.

"Exactly." Wendy nodded. "If there's no threat, then there's no need to attack. If there is, then we'll be ready."

Tiger Lily narrowed her amber flecked eyes, but she kept her lips in a tight line. All eyes turned to Peter, waiting for his reaction as it was clear the Chieftess would give no clear opinion. He ran his fingers through his messy hair and sighed.

"Yeah, I think that is our best option," he agreed. "What do you say, Chief?"

Her gaze darted from side to side as if reading her options in the air. "This is your final decision?"

"It is."

"Then you are not an imbecile," she growled. "You are a coward."

Wendy fought the urge to freshen up that bruise on her jaw. But Peter didn't flinch.

Fists clenched in frustration, Tiger Lily stated, "Fine. I will follow your plan, but only because my hands are tied in this!"

With that, the Chieftess whipped around and left the treehouse, letting the door slam behind her.

She followed him to the sturdy upper tree branch he sat on, her heart leaping as she felt the blissful instant of flight straight up to the perch. He smiled briefly when she joined her, but it waned distractedly.

She nudged him. "What's on your mind?"

He shook his head. "It's just talking today it got me… remembering."

"About the feud?"

Folding his hands over bent knees, Peter nodded solemnly. Then he huffed with a smile; Wendy couldn't tell if it came from pain or humor. Maybe it was both.

"We used to be friends, you know," he reminisced, "Hook and me."

Her breath altered. "I didn't know that."

"I never told you?" He raised an eyebrow in surprise. When she shook her head, he went on to explain, "He was a kid, lived between Blind Man's Bluff with his mom and a ship with his dad. When he was on the Island, he used to join us sometimes on adventures."

Wendy tried to imagine a young James Hook playing with the Lost Boys in the jungles of Neverland. It was difficult. "What happened?"

Peter shrugged. "He wanted to grow up. And after his mom was killed, he was with his father a lot more, learning the trade or whatever. But he... he wanted to make Blind Man's Bluff a place where Lost Boys could have a family, grow up if they wanted to. I mean, this life," he looked around at Hangman's Tree, "it's not for everybody, at least not forever. James saw that. So when he offered, some Lost Boys went with him."

"You let them join the pirates?" Wendy questioned, shocked. When she'd met him, Peter suffered from abandonment issues, a struggle he still dealt with but not nearly so much as he used to. Just letting his brothers go like that, watch them grow up, grow old... and either die or become the pirates who loathed him. Maybe that was the reason why he had abandonment issues. Maybe some of the pirates he'd had to face were once Lost Boys who'd forgotten him.

"Yep. Seemed a good idea at the time." He rubbed the gooseflesh on his arms. "And then James met a girl, single mom; married her, became a family... You know the rest."

She swallowed, remembering when he'd told her about the boy Hook had shot, the battle, the explosion.

They died, all of them.

• • •

165

Peter looked ahead of him blankly, grimacing as if something just occurred to him. "James used to never fear time; it was an adventure of his own. But now he fears it above all else… even me."

Without a word, Wendy took his hand. He squeezed hers appreciatively.

Below, she heard a rustle of leaves in the underbrush. *What's that?*

Before she could check, a jingle grabbed her attention as Tinker Bell zipped up, pinched her nose, and sat on Peter's shoulder. He greeted the fairy with a smile. She pinched his chin.

Turning back to Wendy, Peter said, "You know I was thinking, there's only one problem with your plan: if any of us step foot in Blind Man's Bluff, we're busted. Panther, Lost Boy, fairy, me and you."

Tink laughed. "You seriously underestimate me."

"The past few times you were there, you've been caught, mistaken for an insect, and gotten so drunk you couldn't fly straight."

Face and glow reddening, she muttered, "Of all the things you remember…"

Wendy grinned. "Leave it to me."

*****

Smee found him on the floor of the captain's quarters, empty bottles of rum littering the ground like sea slugs. In his good hand, the Captain held another, arm swiveling side to side. He was staring at something in a cage of iron and glass, something alive and shifting with no mass or form.

"Captain?" Smee questioned, bushy white eyebrows scrunched together.

He took a swig from his bottle, gave a sigh, the bloodshot veins in his blue eyes like blood and sea. "Tell me, Smee; how hard is it to catch a shadow?"

"Nigh near impossible, I'd say," Smee responded, picking up bottles and tucking them under his arm.

"Impossible, you say," he muttered. He ran his claw down the glass face of the cage, making the darkness inside shift and flinch. "Then how do you do it, Smee? How do you catch a shadow?"

Smee nearly dropped the bottles in his arms, hustling to set them in the wooden case built into the wall. "Beats me, Captain. You're the one who'd done it."

"You make a deal with the devil, and then you lure it, make it come of its own will and catch it like an animal," Hook growled, tapping the iron sealing. Then he took another swig of rum. "All you need is bait, you see, Smee? Live and irresistible bait."

"Like the girl, Captain?"

"Aye, Smee. Our little Wendy Bird."

Smee continued tidying the cabin, shaking out a wrinkled shirt. "Too bad she got away; eh, Captain?"

"I'll get her again…"

He chuckled to himself, picking up the dropped or left out food before the rats could try to have at it. "I know you will, Captain." Unable to find a suitable place to put the scraps, Smee shrugged and devoured them. No use in wasting good food.

"And how do you destroy a man, any man, a boy even?" Hook took another gulp of rum, eyes darkening as he stared transfixed on his prisoner. "You take the one he loves and you destroy her, nay, you make certain it's *he* who destroys her. And you let him live with it and suffer after you've turned his dearest against him and take her away for good..." He huffed a drunken humorless laugh at the irony. "But how do you do it, Smee? How do you control a man, make him destroy himself?"

Mouth full and greasy, Smee shook his head. "I don't know, Captain."

Hook downed the last of his rum, eyes of blood and sea unblinking. "You take his shadow."

*****

The sun rose and the screaming stopped. Kai groaned, rubbing his face. No chance of sleep last night, but for maybe two hours he was able to grab it as dawn came and the mouth of Skull Rock drained. Now he sat at the beach, staring helplessly at the expanse of water between him and Neverland's jungles. It wasn't far, but with his ankle still bound by his split, he couldn't swim it.

A chill went down his spine.

"Why didn't you tell me?" he questioned without turning around.

Sylvia stood beside him. "You'd never asked. You didn't need to know then."

"And now?"

She didn't answer.

Kai shook his head. "I need to get off this rock. I can't stay here."

"I agree."

He looked at her then, taken back.

"You must return to your friends," she continued. "They're about to waltz right into trouble. But you can't go

● ● ●
168

now; a path will appear when the tide lowers, stones that go straight across the channel."

"You'll let me go?"

Sylvia nodded.

A huge burden seemed to have lifted from his shoulders. He wasn't going to stay prisoner of the undead. He could finally find the others. Then he frowned, glancing at the woman who stood beside him. Why would she let him go? If she wanted him to help them, to save them, then why would she just let him go without any confirmation or reason to believe that he would even try to release them?

"How can you be his wife?" Kai asked, finding it hard to imagine the villain he'd heard of with Sylvia.

But she didn't change expression. "James isn't the same man I knew him to be. Vengeance destroyed that man, made him forget the good in him and his life."

He ran a hand through his hair, still not sure he could believe her. Could someone like Hook have good in him? But what Long John had said... Perhaps there were some things that turned good men into monsters.

Sylvia sat down, looked right at him and cocked her head. "Who's Gerda?"

A lump the size of a fist swelled up in his throat and his scar got itchy. He could've said a million things about who Gerda was, and yet not one thing fit her in utter completeness. "She's my best friend."

"She's the one you saw when the siren drew you in," Sylvia guessed.

Kai didn't answer. She was right, of course. Blast it, he hated how that sea witch was able to tempt him so easily. How idiotic could he be? Neverland was probably one of the last places Gerda would be, yet one look and he'd fallen for it. Then, to torcher him further, that creature kept her face, *Gerda's* face, so he would forever see her dead face lurking behind his eyelids. Still, he had no one to blame but himself. He'd walked right into the trap.

Then Sylvia smiled sadly, examining him. "You were going to propose to her."

The ring against his chest seemed heavy then, so heavy. But Kai nodded solemnly, unable to form words.

"What a beautiful meadow... *smultronställe*..."

His head snapped up. "How do you know that name?"

"You both loved to visit there, a world of your own that no one else could penetrate," she continued, her voice distant, her eyes looking at something in the air. "But that day, that day someone did. And you never got to ask her."

Vision blurring, Kai choked back tears. *How does she know?*

Sylvia's gaze focused on him, and he knew she didn't need any insight to know what she said next: "You blame yourself."

He passed a hand over his face as if that would help compose himself. But there was no use in denying it. "Everyday."

She was silent a moment, reading him. But he didn't think it was the same kind of thing the siren had done, picking apart his innermost thoughts to manipulate him. This was different. He wasn't sure why.

"You can't live with regret, Kai. If you do, soon that's all you know, all you remember. And that's a sorry life to live." Sylvia's voice changed, her tone pleading, desperate. "I've seen what revenge does to someone. It ruins you. It ruins everyone around you. If you continue the path you're on…"

"This isn't just about revenge," Kai cut in, "not anymore."

"Good."

He resisted the urge to grab the ring, check if it was safe. It was a useless impulse. He knew it was there. He could feel it bumping against the spot near his heart that sometimes matched the chill of his scar.

The pain from these memories showed in his voice despite his best intentions, "How do you do it? How do you know all these things? Gerda, *smultronställe*…"

"It's part of our curse," Sylvia interrupted. Brushing dark curls out of her face, she explained solemnly, "We see everything you all forget. All the happiness, all the pain, everything that simply slips away."

"Everything?"

"Aye, from everyone in Neverland," she affirmed, looking away toward the Island. "That's the real reason they're all afraid to come here. It's because they risk remembering all they forgot. Aye, the beauty, but the ugliness too."

It clicked, then, what it was Kai would see whenever a ghost would touch him. They were memories, the forgotten ones that Sylvia spoke of.

Before he could say anything, she turned to him, so close he started to feel her bone chilling aura. "Let me show you something."

He didn't protest, but he wasn't sure he was prepared for it when her hand went through his and the split second of breath stealing ice that split through him. Then the memory came, sharp and clear as if he were really there:

He walked through the door, such satisfaction at finally returning home after being away filling his chest. He didn't even have time to remove his scarlet coat before the boys found him, rushing at him like a hurricane. Laughter filled the room. All five of them wrestled to greet him. Scooping up the youngest, he cheerfully hoisted the child to sit on his shoulders, earning a few pleadings for the others to have a go.

Then a woman came into the room, a bundle in her arms. She beamed. He felt a glow inside at the sight. He kissed her, longer even after the boys choked in protest. She laughed, pushed him away. Bending over, he kissed the babe in her arms and adjusted the pendant around her neck, so glad to be home and with his family at last.

When Sylvia pulled away, the pain wasn't so bad as it had been before. But the memory ran through his head again, wondering at what he'd seen.

"It was you," Kai realized, blinking. "And... and the man..."

"Was James, yes," Sylvia confirmed. "That was before he tried to save the Lost Boy from being murdered, but then accidently shot him in the scuffle; before the battle and the feud."

Kai shook his head. "Why doesn't he come here? He could see you at any time."

She smiled sadly. "Sometimes the good memories are just as painful as the bad ones."

"Then why stay?"

"It doesn't hurt so much here."

● ● ●

172

The water was slowly receding. Each moment its reach shortened, and Kai thought he could almost see the very tops of the rock path leading to the main Island. It wasn't safe yet to cross with his bad ankle. But he itched with anticipation. Then he realized he still hadn't given an answer to the ghosts' plea for help. Did he even have one?

Why overthink it? The decision has already been made. With the echo of Long John's tales, and every howl of anguish in the bowls of the cave, and Sylvia's explanations at last that pulled everything together... he realized he already knew his decision. Long John had been right: now he cared.

"Sylvia," he vowed at last, "if it is within my power, I will do what I can to help free you from this prison."

She actually smiled, and for a moment he was afraid she would hug him. Instead, she nodded in thanks. "Your word is enough for now. It gives us hope."

Hope. Kai fought a chill of déjà vu. *Perhaps that can be enough for all of us.* But in his experience, he wasn't so sure.

Sylvia stood, facing the ocean. "In a few moments the tide will lower enough for you to cross. But before you go, there are a few things I should tell you." She swallowed uneasily, as if the words were too heavy for her. "James is in way over his head. He's made a deal to help him achieve his revenge even as he doesn't realize what it will cost him."

He felt a chill, recognizing the signs. Is this the same situation as the Queen of Hearts? Did Hook sell his soul to the same master? Then it dawned on him.

"He's after Wendy."

"Not just Wendy anymore, I'm afraid." She looked down at him. "Word has reached him. He knows about your friends, that they're all at Hangman's Tree. He's determined not to fail again."

The word hit him hard. "Again?"

"How do pirates manage to breach a haven that they never could before? Why do they just capture the heart of Pan instead of killing her on the spot? Why take her to her home country over another realm? How does she escape a crew itching to slit her throat? Is it chance? Is it carelessness?" Sylvia questioned, one after the other without pause. "Or could it be something bigger?"

His heart pounded in his throat. *It's all planned.*

Raking his fingers through his hair as the information settled down on him, Kai scowled as he realized, "How does Hook know that Wendy's back? And that they're all at Hangman's Tree; how does he know?"

She ignored his question, nodding towards the channel. "There; it's time."

"How does he know?" he demanded, struggling to his feet.

"You have to go, before the water rises."

"Is there a spy? A spy in Hangman's Tree?"

She froze, lips pursed, back stiff.

That's it. There is a spy.

Brown eyes turned to him, more alive than he'd ever seen them. "Don't hurt her. Promise me. Don't let anything happen to her."

Kai's gut churned, aware that the look in her eyes meant that she would tear his soul to pieces if he didn't do as she said no matter what it cost her. He nodded hesitantly. "I promise." How many times was he going to make promises he wasn't certain he could keep?

"Good," she sighed. "Now go!"

Though his ankle protested, Kai waded up to the first rock and climbed up, taking it slow and careful as he leaped from stone to stone. They were large enough for him to stand without much fear of falling off. He just prayed he wouldn't slip.

A shout sounded behind him, loud and guttural. He turned around to find Long John standing beside Sylvia on Skull Rock's beach far behind him. With a tight smile, Kai waved his hand in farewell. Long John shook his cane at him.

"YOU'D BLOODY WELL KEEP YOUR PROMISE!" the ghost bellowed. "ELSE I'LL PERSONALLY HAUNT YOU FOR THE REST OF YOUR BLASTED DAYS!"

Kai cupped his hands over his mouth. "THAT'D BE PUNISHMENT FOR THE BOTH OF US!"

Long John smirked.

Continuing on again, he tried to concentrate on the staggering path before him.

Don't slip; keep moving; quick, hurry!

The rocks were starting to submerge again when Kai finally got close enough to wade to shore. He sighed in relief, the jungle looming before him in welcome. But he paused, turned back to Skull Rock.

No one was there.

CHAPTER SEVENTEEN
BLIND MAN'S BLUFF

"You're sure we can pass for pirates?"

"We look the part," Alice assured him, resisting the urge to mess with the braids in her blonde locks. "We just need to act the part, blend in, lay low, that kind of thing."

Jack scratched at the skull and crossbones flag on his neck irritably. "This tattoo itches."

"You're the one who asked for it!" Red exclaimed in a harsh whisper. "It's not even real!"

"Now stop scratching it," Alice scolded. "Tattoos aren't supposed to flake off."

Obeying reluctantly, he ran his hand through his hair. The dry paint still itched, and his head twitched in a poor attempt to satisfy it.

They paused just outside of Blind Man's Bluff, the jungle concealing them from view. He couldn't shake the shifting in his gut that they were entering the belly of the beast. The noise was chaotic, not a worry about any kind of invasion. Was there a reason? Even so, he was almost anxious to get in there.

"Don't forget your weapon," Red reminded, handing Jack the cutlass. "You have the pistols?"

He patted his long button down jacket where four pistols lay stowed beneath the leather. They weren't too heavy, but the straps agitated the wounds on his back. "Got them right here. What about you two?"

Both grinned, Red raising an eyebrow that made him nervous. She was the only one in full skirts, which surprised him. "This dress isn't just for show. It's the perfect place to conceal all sorts of weapons."

Alice had a large scarf tied around her waist over tight pants, covering her hips. Did she have other weapons, too, besides the two swords strapped to her belt? Was that a pistol in her boot?

Jack raised his eyebrows. "I see."

Somehow that earned him a pinch on the arm and a punch in the shoulder. Taking a deep breath, Jack entered Blind Man's Bluff with a girl on each arm, blending in with the crowd of pirates they plunged into.

Marketers shouted out passersby, beckoning them to purchase their wares. Pubs were packed with hungry men and women, and bars resorted to move outside to take advantage of the surge of people. The docks were busy, bustling with people. A woman, dark skinned with dreads falling to her hips, shoved past them with yards of rigging hooked over her shoulder.

Where do we even start?

Red stole the hat off a snoozing old seadog, plopping it on her own teased up hair. She seemed so natural. Why couldn't he have some of that ease?

"We're getting some attention," she whispered to them. "Alice…"

Jack followed where the girls were looking, noticed the flock of women in loose shirts, tight corsets, and layers of skirts giving them narrow eyed glances. The half-drunk brutes they were hanging off of were looking their way, too, to see what was drawing the ladies' attention.

Blasted bloody—

• • •

Alice and Red exchanged a look. In unison, they clutched tighter to Jack; Alice nearly stumbling over the cobblestones, Red giggling unnaturally. Both openly stared at him, which made him feel awfully uncomfortable, or cast glares at the women who'd turned up their noses.

Jack frowned. "What are you—"

"Shut up and act like a prat," Red hissed between her teeth.

What wise advice, he thought but dared not say.

Puffing out his chest, he pulled on the most arrogant and haughty sneer he could muster. Taking longer strides, he was almost afraid he really was just barely dragging Alice along. The men who'd been watching burst out laughing for whatever reason. Not that it had anything to do with him. His disguise was a smidge from perfection!

When they'd passed the scene, it was getting harder to travel together in all the hustle going on. Alice leaned closer, walking right again, and informed, "It'll take forever to scope things out like this. I'm going to split up, get a wider berth of the situation."

"You sure you're fine on your own?" Jack questioned, looking around, finding alarms everywhere. "It's not exactly the kind of place to be on your own since…"

"Since I'm a girl?"

Jack shrugged, but didn't deny it.

Alice smiled. "I appreciate the concern, but I'll be fine. I'll meet up with you two later. Keep an eye on him, Red."

"Hey!" Jack started offensively.

Red stifled a laugh. With that, Alice parted from the trio, disappearing into the crowds.

● ● ●

Alice slinked into the dark alley, stepping over a man slumped against a wall who reached out for her. She flinched away, noting his empty eye sockets, feeling suddenly sick. But he didn't come after her, so she kept on. Avoiding the rats and a snogging couple in a shadowy corner, she froze when she heard the voices in the crossroads behind the buildings.

"Hey, I've been looking for you," a heavy male voice sounded. "The Captain sent me."

Captain? she pondered. *Like Captain Hook? Was there more than one captain?*

Pressing her back against the wall, she kept her ear close to the wall's edge. From the corner of her eye, she could see them.

"What happened to your face?" questioned another pirate, tall and cleaner with short cropped hair and onyx skin.

The first was stocky and bald, tattoos crawling up his browned head. He touched the large welt on his temple, half of his left eye scarlet. "Cruddy Lost Boy knocked me out with a sorry excuse for a staff."

"Mustn't have been too sorry of a staff if it did its job," the first quipped with a grin.

Alice's heart skipped a beat. *Borogove.*

This had to be one of those pirates Jack had encountered in the jungle. Hopefully he'd never seen his attacker's face, or at least didn't remember it.

"Anyway, the Captain's waiting for your response." The stocky pirate scowled, changing the subject. "So what'll it be, Jones? You staying or going?"

Going where?

• • •

"Bill Jukes," Jones sighed, rubbing the back of his head, "I've been a friend of Hook's since we were training on the same ship as lads. But I have a family, now. I won't put them in danger. I can't get into any war."

"There'll be a war whether you stay or go," Bill Jukes said gruffly. "Those little devils are sure to attack sooner than if you come with us. Fighting where we're going isn't supposed to come for a while."

"Yeah, but the way I see it, there's a definite in that war that you're getting into. Here, it's only a possibility."

War...

"Why's your ship set to sail, then?"

"I'm taking my family and whoever else is staying back to the boarder," Jones explained, tugging on his coat lining. "It's safer there. No Lost Boys, no Panthers, and no mysterious war."

Bill Jukes groaned, "I'm not gonna lie, Jones, the Captain was really hoping you'd join the fleet. He's not gonna like this."

"Hook has more important things to worry about than me. Send him my regards, though."

Jones turned to go, Bill Jukes calling out, "Will do." He started off the opposite direction.

She paused a moment, trying to make sense of what she'd witnessed. The gathering, it wasn't just that. All the pirates, all the ships coming in; Hook was forming an armada. Where was he going? Where would he need a fleet? What war was he preparing for?

There were only two options she could think of, why the armada and the war and the gathering: Hook was going to strike the Panther Tribe, their camp being on the coast—but that was unlikely, as the cliffs were impenetrable and too high to attack from the ocean—or he was making an escape from Neverland. Alice shivered. She had to warn the others. Hook was another pawn for the force they've been looking for.

Turning away from the wall to run back down the alley, she ran right into someone. Hands grabbed her by the shoulders to stop her stumbling. Pale eyes glinted in the dim light.

"Hello, there," the man sneered, standing over a head taller than her. "What's a pretty lass like you doing way back here?"

"I must've missed a turn," Alice lied, trying to back away.

He didn't let go, keeping her pinned against the wall. Her heart raced.

"Please let me go, sir," she said as evenly as she could, trying to calm herself.

"Sir?" He cocked his head. His breath smelled heavily of liquor. "No woman's ever called me *sir* before."

Too close, too close!

Without another moment to contemplate, she kicked her knee up between his legs and stomped down hard on his foot. He started to howl, stepping away just enough for her to pop him in the jaw with her elbow. When he still didn't fall, she swung around and grabbed his throat in the pit of her elbow, locking her arm in place. So he couldn't swing her over his head, she wrenched him back and planted a kick at his femur. It didn't take long before the man fell unconscious, dropping out of her hold.

● ● ●

"How's about *drunk pervert*, does that sound more fitting?" Alice shot, propping the pirate against the wall so it wouldn't rouse suspicion. She did take his hat, though.

Brushing off her beige corset and straightening the blue scarf around her waist, she managed to compose herself as best she could before she strutted back down the alley as if nothing had happened. She couldn't get her hand to stop shaking, though.

"Tone it down a bit," Red whispered. "You're drawing to much attention to yourself."

"Yeah, *I'm* the one who's drawing the attention," Jack muttered.

"What's that supposed to mean?"

"Nothing."

Despite knowing the real reason the yellow eyed scoundrels smirked their way, Jack dropped any pretense in his behavior to please Red. He still shot a glare at those yellow eyed scoundrels, though. He didn't want them getting ideas.

"Wait, stop," Red cautioned.

Stumbling to a halt, he waited expectantly. Eyebrows furrowed, gaze fixed on nothing in particular, she seemed to be waiting for something.

"What is it?" he asked.

"I heard something."

"What'd you hear?"

She shushed him, looking over her shoulder. "Follow my lead. Act casual."

Before he could question it, she steered him around back towards an outdoor bar where some pirates were taking a break. He tried not to panic. It was as if Red meant to join them.

Thankfully, she didn't. She led him to an inconspicuous corner within earshot of the chatting group, turning back to him with two rum bottles in her hand.

Jack's mouth nearly fell open. "Where… How…?"

"I have a slick hand," she said simply, offering him a bottle. "Now drink."

He took it skeptically. "You drink?"

Red rolled her eyes. "They're empty, blockhead! Now, bottoms up."

"Are you kidding? You don't know where that's been!"

She raised an eyebrow mischievously, looking him dead in the eye as she pressed the bottle to her lips and took a swig as if there were liquor inside.

He wrinkled his nose. "You did that just to spite me."

A smile tugged at her mouth. She inclined the bottle his way, indicating it was his turn.

Making me drink from a nasty used rum bottle, he thought with a grumble.

When he took a swig of air, bittersweet droplets fell on his tongue. He made a face, forcing himself not to vomit.

He scowled. "Nasty."

Red laughed, pretending to take another sip. He decided it wasn't worth another go. Pressing a finger to her lips, she jerked her head subtly to the group behind them. Jack quieted, tuning into the pirates' conversation and watching them over Red's shoulder.

"Blast it; where ye even going?" an old seadog questioned, voice gravelly and difficult to understand. He stood behind the bar, leaning over the counter with a rag in his hand. "Does Hook *ken*? Does anyone?"

"Nah, he doesn't know," a woman huffed, ginger hair braided over one shoulder. "If he does, he hasn't mentioned. All he knows is we'll be rid of those good for nothing Lost Boys and that Pan at last."

"We'll never be rid of those boys, Anney," a large man with a thick black mustache corrected. "Neverland will always be collecting more Lost Boys and there'll always be a Pan. Won't always be Peter Pan, though. The Island will pick a new partner, they say, when the current one's gone."

"How daft!" a girl cried, tossing her curly frizz. "The Island isn't alive, is it?"

Anney rolled her eyes, sipping from her tankard.

"It certainly is, in its own way," the old barman said, wiping out mugs. "Neverland's a life force of its own. It's a reflection of Pan, or whoever its partner is at the time."

"Cookson's right," Mustache agreed.

"Posh," Frizzy puffed, twisting closer to the large pirate. "Let's go back to Hook's big plan. I'm just itching for another adventure. I think it's thrilling, absolutely thrilling! What do you think, Mister Starkey?"

Mister Starkey grinned behind his black mustache. "It'll be an adventure, alright."

"Oh, I wish we could go now!" she pouted. "I can't wait any longer."

"What is keeping the Captain, Starkey?" another pirate questioned, piping in. He stood beside Anney who wasn't paying him the least bit of attention.

"He's waiting for the kid to deliver," Starkey responded. "Soon as he's got the package, we're sailing out o' here."

"Rubbish!" Cookson exclaimed, slapping his cleaned tankard on the bar. "The lot of ye can have yer fun, get yer fair taste of blood and all that. As fer me, I've slit one too many throats in me lifetime. I'll be staying here with Jones and all the others sane enough to stay."

"Awe, you're no fun!" Frizzy teased.

"Mark me words: I was born here, may just as well die here."

"I was neither born here, nor do I plan on dying here," Anney grumbled. "And I certainly don't plan on selling my soul to some puppeteer ready to pull my strings. I'm leaving on the hour with Calico to pillage and plunder like *real* pirates."

"Then you pay for another round, if it's to be your last," Starkey laughed.

Anney raised an eyebrow, pulling her hat on and tossing a handful of doubloons on the counter before she stomped off.

Jack almost didn't catch it when Red took the bottle from his hands and set the both of them on a nearby barrel. "We'd better go," she whispered, "before we get too suspicious."

Grabbing his hand, she dragged him away to fall back into the chaos. He barely had time to collect himself.

"Did you hear those guys?" he gasped, hastening to match her step.

"Of course I did."

"The package?"

• • •

"Whatever it is, we can't let them have it."

"What about the kid?" he stated urgently. "You don't think—"

Someone grabbed his other arm, falling into step with them. "We need to talk," Alice whispered.

Red shook her head. "No, we need to go."

*****

She typically didn't fly this high, not for long anyway. The air got too cold up here without proper attire. Often she'd have to return to lower altitudes, especially flying long distance. But even as crystalized droplets clung to her skin, Wendy didn't let herself worry about such things as she flew over the clouds. The sky exploded into a thousand shades of blue and yellow up here, the sun half swimming in an ocean of white. It was getting harder to breathe. Bumps crawled up her flesh.

Best go back now, she reasoned, *before I'm missed, or pass out from the altitude.*

Leaning forward, she let herself go into freefall, plummeting head first through the layer of clouds, diving through the sky. The jungle rushed up to meet her. Before it was too late, she scooped up and slowed herself, skimming over the treetops until she got to the right place. Wendy lowered herself into a tree and climbed the rest of the way down.

Dropping from the lowest branch, she slipped and stumbled into the creek, soaking her boots.

Of course...

Stomping out of the water, she shook off the mud on the bank.

The bushes rustled behind her. Her heart leaped. Knife out in a flash, she whipped around and sent it flying with the flick of her wrist. The blade whizzed by Peter's head and lodged itself in a tree trunk. Wendy gasped.

"Peter! Sorry, I almost thought…"

"Nah, it's fine." He flashed his dimpled grin, turning to tear the knife from the tree. "I don't blame you, though pirates tend to stray away from this spot. And the Tick Tock is a little lower to the ground…"

Wendy made a face. But she found herself listening out for the monster, now that she realized she stood just a few steps away from Crocodile Creek. Even so, this made for the perfect meeting spot when one wants to avoid pirates not too far from Cannibal Cove.

"Besides, I consider myself lucky," Peter laughed. "If you really meant to hit me, I'd be dead."

"I'm pretty sure there was a compliment in there somewhere in that taunt."

His eyes twinkled.

Two skips towards her, and he bowed deeply, bestowing the blade. "Your knife, milady."

She bit her lip to suppress a giggle, but darn her treacherous smile! She couldn't keep it back. "Thank you, kind sir."

Taking the knife from him, she slid it back into her belt. When she turned back, Peter was standing straight, so close, his eyes making her heart flutter. She smiled back up at him, her face growing warm.

"You forget yourself, sir," she teased, eyes falling briefly to feign bashfulness. Then she realized what she'd said, instantly regretting it.

● ● ●

His gaze never wavered. "I may forget myself, but you I could never forget."

All worries vanished in one moment. She could see her whole world in his eyes. Standing up on her tiptoes, Wendy kissed him light and sweet. It earned a genuine grin, though, the kind that forgot all troubles. He leaned forward as if to kiss her again, but she stopped him.

"Not now, flyboy; we still have a fiend to take care of." She made a face. "Oh goodness, I sound like my father."

The jungle erupted behind them. Wendy snapped out her dagger; Peter whipped around. Then from the underbrush burst Red followed by Alice and Jack, all dirt smudged and out of breath. She sighed in relief, sheathing her blade once more.

"You're back!"

"What'd you find out?" Peter questioned anxiously.

Jack raised his hand briefly, but wasn't making any sense between the wheezing and the gasping.

Red caught her breath first, readjusting her skirt. "The pirates are leaving."

"*Leaving?*" Wendy and Peter questioned in unison.

That doesn't make any sense...

"It's the Master," Alice huffed out between excitement and worry. "Hook's working for him."

"Or her," Jack managed to cut in.

Alice ignored him. "He's forming an armada—"

"But they're waiting for something, a package," Red cut in.

Someone stumbled out of from underbrush in a rush. Wendy barely had time to brace herself before she recognized her. Jane raised her hands up in self-defense, her expression beyond urgent.

"Don't attack! I have something I need to tell you!"

"Don't trust her!" Jack gasped out, pointing accusingly.

Wendy saw the movement just before Jane cried out, an iron claw shooting out of the shadows and held to her throat. Her blood went cold, instinctively going to reach her. But pirates burst out from the jungle, surrounding them instantly. Something shot out overhead, covering the sky for a moment before descending down on them. Ducking down, Wendy covered her head before the net landed. The ropes weighed her down, Peter trapped with her. She looked up just in time to see her friends form a ring around them, swords drawn to protect them.

Peter stood stiffly, the heavy net casting strange shadows over his face. "Hook."

Wendy felt her stomach clench in fear as the Captain stepped out of the dark jungle, blue eyes glinting. "Hello, Pan. Ah, I've missed you."

Jane cringed, the claw pressed dangerously hard against her throat. Cold fear for her stilled Wendy's impulse to draw a weapon.

"Don't hurt her!" she exclaimed with all the demanding force she could muster.

Hook raised an eyebrow. "Surrender your weapons, and we'll see."

"Don't do it," Jack hissed. "It's a trick."

With a cruel grin, Hook gripped her arm firmly. The sharp claw pierced her skin, blood running down her throat. Jane's jaw tightened, breathing quickened.

Without a word, Wendy removed the daggers in her boots and the sword at her side, dropped them on the ground. Peter did the same, stone faced.

"Let her go," he barked. "It's me you want."

Hook shrugged, releasing his hold. Jane stumbled away, breathing quickly in shock. She didn't run off…

Something's wrong.

"Jane?" Peter questioned, confusion in his tone too.

Jane touched her bleeding throat, pulling away and staring at her blood.

Red scowled. "I knew it. She's the spy."

"Spy?" Wendy frowned, the word shooting through her.

Brown eyes looked up, met hers for a brief moment, fell on Peter. Then her expression hardened, and she turned away, snatching a rag from a nearby pirate and holding it to her wound. Confusion was replaced by hurt inside Wendy's gut.

"You betrayed us…"

Hook laughed. "You can blame Pan for it! You're not his only weakness, Miss Darling, and you're not his first either."

Her throat knotted. Jane wouldn't look at them.

Peter's hands were shaking. "This whole time…"

Jane's eyes snapped up. Wendy felt like she'd been shot. They were so different, fiercer, harder, angrier.

"You killed my mother," Jane said between clenched teeth as if every word were a dagger. "I don't judge you for your loyalty to your family, Pan. Just don't judge me for my loyalty to mine."

● ● ●

It dawned on her then, in growing dreadful realization. "You're his daughter," she guessed, the idea still settling.

Jane didn't flinch, but Hook laid a hand on her shoulder and affirmed, "My own flesh and blood."

"Alright, I guessed the spy thing, but this I didn't see coming," Jack disclosed.

The Captain raised his claw, a signal. With a rush of rope, the net yanked Wendy back and snatched her feet out from under her, knocking her into Peter where they both fell to the ground. She caught one glance at Peter's face, pained and angry, before the pirates pulled their entrapment again and dragged them across the jungle floor. Shouts from her friends caught her ear. Amongst the tumble, she thought she saw the pirates struggle to overcome them. Then all was dirt and leaves and bruising ground, and Peter squashed against her, and ropes rubbing into her skin.

What's more, no one knows where we are or what's happened.

The clearing was soon vacant, silent save for the water gushing down the creek. Unusual for the jungle to be so quiet, even this close to Cannibal Cove. But then the ticking came, faint and growing, louder and louder. The Crocodile that crawled into the space reeking of humans, metal, and gunpowder was monstrous. There wasn't a beast on the Island that didn't stay out of his way. A massive head swung this way and that, searching for unfortunate victims. Finding none, he loped over the bank and slinked into the creek, the ticking in his throat muffled under the water. He swam for Cannibal Cove, sensing a battle brewing somewhere in his

● ● ●

stomach. No hard work necessary for a meal when there was a fight. All he had to do was wait patiently for blood to spill. Battles never failed him.

CHAPTER EIGHTEEN
LATE ARRIVAL

As soon as Kai stumbled into the clearing, he knew he'd run into dangerous territory. In a scramble—as if they were shocked by his sudden appearance—a hoard of masked and painted figures surrounded him. Skidding to a stop, Kai's hands shot up in truce. Weapons shot out, aimed at him in all manors. Even slingshots were drawn and clubs poised threateningly.

"I'm a friend! Don't attack!" Kai exclaimed, trying to make sense of the scene, realizing these were Lost Boys and tribesmen. Thinking quickly, he added, "I need to see Pan."

"Pan's not here," a Lost Boy with an owl mask called out.

"Wendy, then; let me speak to her," he implored urgently. He wasn't sure how much time he had to get to them. "Jack, Red, Alice? Anyone; I need to see them."

"HOLD YOUR FIRE!" the booming command jarred through the crowd. Kai saw the kid who'd said it, a bear mask covering his brown face.

Then came another bark, female, not quite as loud but infinitely more stabbing.

Weapons lowered, some more hesitant than others. The swarm shuffled back to make room for those who elbowed their way to the center. Kai made a note of each of them: the large boy with the bear mask, twin raccoon faced kids, a small boy with black messy hair, a tall boy with his mask pushed up over orange hair, a kid with pearly round teeth, and a young woman with amber flecked eyes and feathers in her teased hair. He tried to remember their names from when Wendy had told him about them.

"Who're you?" His eyes narrowed—Slightly, wasn't it? It had to be. His hands were fidgeting. "You don't look like any kid."

"Or Native Neverlandian for that matter," added the toothy one. What was his name?

"I'm Kai, a friend of Wendy's. I came with her and three others here, but we got—"

"Separated," put in one Twin.

"We know," added the other.

Kai furrowed his brow. "Then where are they?"

Tiger Lily—there was no question of who she was—looked him up and down, stone faced. She didn't respond, though it felt like she had plenty to say about the situation.

"Jane had gone earlier to check on them, but it's been all morning and no one's come back," explained the kid... Nibs! That was it.

Wait, what is going on here?

"Check on them? What's happening?"

They hesitated, as if they were still debating whether to trust him or not. He didn't have time for this! And with every second he felt an impending sense of dread rise in his stomach.

"What is going on?" he urged.

Removing his mask, Curly made a face of final contemplation before he explained, "Your friends were sent into Blind Man's Bluff to spy and whatnot. Peter and Wendy were supposed to meet them near Crocodile Creek when they thought they got enough information to figure out why the pirates are gathering and what we should do about it."

"And?"

He shrugged. "We haven't heard from them yet."

Raking a hand through his hair, Kai's mind raced. "You said you sent someone to check on them?"

Slightly nodded. "Jane left a while ago."

"Who's Jane?"

"Lost girl."

The dread rose dramatically. "How long ago did she leave?"

"I don't know. Long while, I guess."

Kai cursed, stamping his foot down in frustration. *I'm too late! I wasn't fast enough.*

Tiger Lily raised an eyebrow. "You do not sound surprised."

"I'm frustrated!" he exclaimed, the reality of the situation dawning on him. "I couldn't warn them in time. And now they're all probably—*nej*, definitely captured by Hook."

"Captured?" Curly questioned, the word making the surrounding group shift and mutter.

The Twins stepped closer, pine eyes glinting behind their raccoon masks. "How would you know?"

"The girl, she's a spy; don't you see?" Kai insisted.

Slightly frowned. "Jane?"

"She's working for Hook, and she just made the perfect trap! With my friends in the pit of pirates, and their meeting place so close where both Wendy *and* Pan would meet them; all she'd need to do is tell the Captain to lie in wait, then volunteer to check on the group so as not to rouse suspicion. Or just to buy some time." He cursed again in Swedish, hating how easy it must've been.

• • •

Eyes narrowed skeptically all around. Of course they doubted him! But he didn't have time for this. If Hook was going to take them away...

A bright light zipped up out of nowhere, stopping directly in front of him. Blinking away the blinding spots staining his vision, he recognized the form of a fairy inside the light. She glared at him.

Harsh bells jangled when she opened her mouth. He wasn't so sure it was a pretty phrase.

"How do we know *you're* not working for Hook?" Nibs translated.

Tinker Bell nodded sharply, affirming the translation.

Kai didn't flinch, but his voice lowered considerably. "You don't. But if you don't believe me, then point me in the direction of Blind Man's Bluff and I'll go find them myself."

She rattled off again, and Nibs interpreted, "If you're right, then they'd be expecting you and you'd be killed or caught within a crocodile's length of the docks."

"Try me."

Pinching her lips, she thought it over before she gave a quick ring. Nibs made a face. "I don't think I'll translate that. The gist of it is: she believes you."

Kai nodded in thanks, hoping the word of a pixie was worth more than he'd anticipate.

Of course, the group exploded into thousands of questions and exclamations in chaotic confusion. None were directed at anyone in particular, just open air wondering what to do... without Pan. It was practically impossible to think straight. Even Tiger Lily seemed frazzled.

Then the one kid, the only one who hadn't spoken, stepped forward. Tootles looked directly up at him, eyes

• • •

196

large and old, much too old for a child. "Can you get them back?"

Kai nodded grimly. "I can try."

"Will you lead us?"

"Lead?" Tiger Lily growled. "Your government is so unstable without Pan that you would entrust a stranger to lead you on a rescue mission?"

"Government?" Slightly laughed like the very notion was preposterous. "All we've got is Pan, and he's captured. Do you see any other leaders about?"

"I am Chieftess!"

"Eh, doesn't really qualify to us Lost Boys."

"No offense," the Twins chirped.

Tiger Lily ignored them, raising an accusing finger at Kai. "And he *qualifies?*"

"Tootles thinks so," Curly spoke up. "And he hardly says anything he thinks unless it's important."

"Tink, too," Nibs chimed in. "Well, not the last bit. I'm not sure she can help saying what she thinks."

Tink rattled off a few chimes that made him cringe.

Grinding her teeth, Tiger Lily glared at all of them. But she didn't say another word about it.

The matter seeming to have settled—or at least as far as the Lost Boys were concerned—they all turned to Kai expectantly. His mind raced, pieces coming together in his head. Would it work? Most likely Hook would be expecting retaliation.

He's expecting the retaliation of a child, or the strike from a tribe, he realized. But maybe... maybe he won't be expecting an attack from a pirate.

• • •

Kai's heart pounded with anticipation. "Alright, here's the plan."

CHAPTER NINETEEN

EVERYTHING IS A CHOICE

Iron cuffs clamped around her wrists, bound behind her back and bolted to the ship's floor at the end of a heavy chain barely long enough to let her stand. But her body hurt so terribly that her muscles only just allowed her to sit up on aching knees. Wendy's head snapped at the cruel laughter, blinking in the brig's dim light. Pirates were busy binding someone just in front of her.

Peter.

She struggled up to get closer, but the chain pulled her back down. They were tying him to an anchor, obviously tugging the knots tighter than necessary. Peter cringed, just as beat up from the drag through the jungle as she was. The taunting multiplied, sneering at him, showing him who was in control.

Then came the first kick right in the ribs. Wendy was too shocked to do anything, but it jarred through her. Then they hit him again. And again. And again.

"Stop it!" Wendy shouted desperately.

They didn't pay her any attention.

Peter gave a cry at a throw to the knee.

"STOP IT!" she screamed. Anxious, she repeated it at the top of her lungs, followed by a string of insults she'd never used before. None of it had any effect.

The beating continued in brute sequence, over and over, until someone landed a blow to the head. He lay limp, his position unnatural as he was still pinned to the anchor. Wendy waited, frozen, to see if he was conscious. Thankfully, he blinked with such forceful repetition he had to be struggling against passing out.

She bit back tears. Agh, she hated this! Stuck to the side while he was being beaten, unable to do anything except scream. It hurt more than anything else.

The pirates at last backed off, but she realized it wasn't because of sympathy. Looking up, she saw a figure descending the stairs from the above deck.

Jane.

She looked different. With her leather coat and tall boots, she looked every inch the pirate she was. At the same time, she looked like the same Jane. That's what made it worse.

When Peter saw her, he grimaced as if he'd been punched in the gut again. "You filthy traitor," he growled.

"Now, now," said the rotund Mister Smee who followed Jane down with a torch, "no need to call names."

Before she said anything, Jane approached Wendy with a dagger in hand. Peter shouted in protest. Unable to react, she barely flinched when the blade touched her neck briefly and something snapped. Jane held the bronze acorn in her hand.

"No more happy thoughts," she muttered, pocketing the trinket.

Wendy's heart sank.

When Jane stepped over to Peter, stone faced, he spat, "We took you in, accepted you, called you sister…"

"Don't blame me for your bad judgement," Jane said evenly, relieving him of his thimble quickly, then backed away.

"You betrayed us!"

"And you owe me!"

The phrase echoed through the brig.

Wendy scowled. "He owes you nothing."

"He owes me everything," Jane shot back. "My mother, my life, my *father*. My whole life has revolved around you, Pan. Every day was spent in preparation for facing you, every nightmare growing up had you lurking in the shadows, every waking moment my father has been *obsessed* with you! And ever since I've come back to this island, you have been around every corner of my existence."

Peter looked up at her grimly. "I can't give you back your mother, or your life up to now, or your father's sanity. The debt you claim is impossible to pay!"

"Then I will make you *pay* for it."

Wendy's gut churned. Jane was too calm, too sure of herself. She had the cool steel that Hook lacked, making her just as unpredictable, maybe even more so dangerous.

Breathing heavily, Peter glowered at her. The anchor's weight made him hunched and the shadows fell over his eyes. "So you're going to kill me? Just like that?"

Jane cocked her head curiously, bending down on one knee to look him in the eye. "I don't want to kill you. I want to *destroy* you."

Her heart pounded rapidly.

"And the way I'm going to destroy you, Pan," Jane continued, swinging her arm back to point at Wendy, "is by

• • •

destroying her. And she can know it was your fault for all her pain and loss just before we kill her."

"No!"

She smiled. "Your reaction only proves my point."

Standing, Jane turned to face Wendy. She did her best to hold her chin high despite her ability to only kneel. Peter struggled and gave a bark of angry protest, but a pirate standing by bashed him in the stomach, making him keel over in breathless agony.

Jane whirled on the pirate who'd hurt him. "Did I ask you to strike him?!"

He scowled. "'e was ask'n for it."

"I don't care if *he* was asking for it; did *I* ask you for it?"

The pirate sneered in response.

She stepped towards him. "Next time you try that again, Mullins, you might just as well kill him. See how the Captain appreciates you taking what's his."

That comment made him hang his head, step away from Peter with a pout. Wendy noticed how Jane released her clenched fist. Was she trying to hide something? Prove something? Turning back to Wendy, Jane's expression was cool and collected, but her eyes were iron. Whatever soft spot she might have had for Peter—if indeed what she suspected was true—it did not extend to Wendy.

"Mother to the Lost Boys," Jane listed evenly, approaching her one step at a time like a leopard, "Heart of the Pan, practically nemesis to the Chieftess, Bane of the pirates; the Bird, Wendy Moira Angela Darling." Stopping directly in front of her, she looked down with disappointed distaste. "I expected more."

"Names are powerful things," Wendy said calmly. "Be cautious in how you use them."

"Ah, I almost forgot your mastery of words." She stooped down, just barely out of reach. She still smelled of the sandalwood that floored the treehouse in Hangman's Tree. "But I have a story for you, Bird. There's a house in Bloomsbury, London, England; a corner house where there's a view of the great clock tower in the nursery."

Pulse quickening, Wendy felt a hollow pit form in her abdomen.

"A man and woman with hair gone grey and lines etching their faces live there, waiting for any news from the authorities that perhaps they've found their daughter. Aye, they think her strange, perhaps. But the woman is beginning every day to believe the strange stories her daughter spoke of; and at night when her husband falls asleep on the living room chair waiting for a call from the investigators, she will go up to that precious little nursery where her grandchildren now doze and watch the stars above that clock tower. She keeps the window open, always open. And she prays to God to return her daughter or keep her safe wherever she may be. But even though her husband still thinks the notion preposterous, she also begs to the stars to send a message to the boy, that angel boy, to keep her daughter safe. *Find her,* she pleads, *and let me see her again, please, or let me know she's safe.* But mostly, she tends to the nightlights, makes sure they shine bright in case she should fall asleep and they must take over watching the grandchildren and looking for the daughter who was taken should she return."

Jane cocked her head. "Shall I tell you about the man, now? He doesn't beg so much as his wife, and he doesn't

* * *

cave to the fantasies. But every morning before he goes to work, he pops on his hat and lops over to the police station to make sure those inspectors keep up their job. Then on his way home from work, he stops by again just in case any developments have occurred while he's been busy. Sometimes he's civil and professional, a curious regular. But other times he shouts at the amateurs because they've been so unsuccessful, and he slams the door behind him upon exiting. He never cries, though. The crying doesn't come until he sits on that living room chair beside the hand cranked telephone."

Tears carved lines down Wendy's face. Her throat swelled in anguish and anger. She wanted to run to her parents, let them know she was alright, comfort them, ease their worried hearts. But she also sensed a threat in the midst of Jane's stories.

How does she know so much about my family?

Jane smiled. "Now, John's really made something of himself. He knows so much about things like stocks and shares, just like his old man. He visits his parents frequently, but his wife makes sure he still balances time with the children and work. Life must continue. They still pray every night around the dinner table for his dear sister, and when tucking his kids to bed and they ask him what happened to their aunt, he smiles sadly because he doesn't want his worry on them. So instead he tells them stories that his sister used to tell him, tells them their aunt was on an adventure. *Where?* they ask. *I believe she called it Never Never Land,* he responds. *When will she be back?* they continue. That's when he shrugs. *I don't know.*"

"How do you know this?" Wendy heaved, unable to keep the pain and rage out of her voice.

• • •

She ignored her question. "And Michael, hasn't he just recently had his second child? A daughter called Margaret, I believe. Funny, that's my middle name." Her dark eyes shone in the dim light. "He's still such a young father. Moved his little family in with his parents to look after them. The kids keep the joy in the house, not to mention the cook on her toes. Did you know that old Liza's still working there? They like to pretend their dog, Porthos, is a circus bear. And Michael confesses to his wife that sometimes he thinks he can remember things that shouldn't be possible. American Natives and glowing insects and a flying pirate ship... But he's never been to America, and fireflies don't jingle like bells, and pirate ships aren't supposed to fly. He must be dreaming, she insists. But it feels like more than a dream. It's almost like a memory. Maybe when his sister comes back, he can ask her about it. If she comes back."

"Why are you telling me this?"

"I'm telling you this so you know what you left behind."

That jarred through her with such accusation she felt like the iron Jane portrayed. Wendy ground her teeth. "I didn't leave them. I was *taken*. And when I see them again, I will explain everything."

"You won't have the chance."

"If you hurt my family, there is nothing that will stop me from getting to you."

"Oh, I'm not going to hurt them." Jane jerked her head back to Peter. "He is."

Peter gave a sharp laugh, splitting the air and making every pirate—especially Smee—jump back with a start. He leaned his head back to prop against the anchor, looking over his nose at Jane. "That's your plan? Do your worst to me! You can't control me."

Then came a chuckle, making her skin crawl. Buckled boots stomped down the stairs. The shifting light glinted off the golden buttons on his scarlet coat.

"*You can't control me*, he says," Hook mimicked as he came down. "Tell me, Pan, how often have you told that lie?"

"Hook, you old codfish; come to join the party?" Peter mocked.

"How do you control a Pan? How is it done?"

"You always were full of rhetorical questions. Comes with the dramatic effect."

"You capture the darkest part of any man, the place where you store the blackest bits of your soul." Hook stepped between them, swinging an empty lantern. But it wasn't empty. Holding it up with his claw, he snatched a torch from Smee, the firelight illuminating his features. "And you shine a light under it."

The flames flicked up to the lantern and the *darkness* inside recoiled. Peter screamed. Hook grinned. And then the Island groaned deep in its very core, the sound reverberating through the ship and rattling the waves.

"Stop it!" Wendy cried, the pieces beginning to fit together despite her desperation.

Jane stood quickly, turning toward her father but he'd already removed the torch. Peter calmed, and the shifting Shadow within the lantern hesitantly returned to its former state. The Island too ceased its retaliation.

Peter panted heavily, eyes wide. "How…?"

● ● ●

"Come now, did you really think I'd go through so much trouble just to kidnap your little Wendy?" Hook raised an eyebrow, lowering the lantern to his side again. The entire company seemed to hold their breath in wait to see what would happen next.

Does he really have the power to control Peter? Wendy wondered with growing dread. *Or is he unknowingly severing the ties between Pan and Neverland?*

Hook's eyes glittered. "Don't worry, that's about as much as I can do for now. Soon, though, I will control you, Pan. Or else, I won't have to."

Turning on his heel, he began to take his leave again, ascending the stairs with the rest of the pirates moving to follow.

"All roads lead to one thing, Pan: you. Only you." He paused a moment as if the idea had struck him suddenly. "And that's what terrifies you the most."

Then he disappeared, and the rest filed after. Jane was all that remained. She looked at Peter, and for the first time Wendy thought she finally saw her for who she was: torn between the Pan and the Hook. Conflicted. Alone.

"I'm sorry," Jane whispered. Then she turned away, hiding her face.

But Peter snapped up. He wasn't finished with her yet.

"Listen to me, Jane. *LISTEN!*" he shouted, demanding her attention. "Everything you do, *EVERYTHING* is a choice. And every choice has consequences."

She hesitated, glanced back at him over her shoulder. "I made my choice a long time ago."

• • •

He glowered, eyes darkened. "Then I hope you can live with the consequences."

Jane grimaced. But still, she made to follow after the pirates to the upper decks.

Not so fast, Wendy thought, mind racing.

"Sister to the Lost Boys," she called, her words stopping Jane in her tracks, "Traitor to the Pan, daughter of the Hook, betrayer of friends, liar to herself; forever the Lost Girl: Jane Margaret Hook." Wendy breathed deeply, lowering her voice like a curse. "You will never be content."

Lips in a thin line, Jane hastened up the stairs, sealing the trapdoor behind her. In the black and blue of the brig again, Peter recovering from the pain of his injuries, Wendy slumped over. What was going to happen now?

*****

Fingering the wooden pendent at her neck, Jane tried to calm herself. It'd belonged to her mother, or at least, she thought so. Her memories were still muggy in certain areas.

Mother.

She closed her eyes, trying to imagine her. But she couldn't conjure up a picture however hard she tried. They had the same eyes, she was told. That's it. And she dared not question her father about it, afraid it would send him into a frenzy. Whether in anger or despair, it didn't matter. She couldn't do that to him, not purposefully.

Gosh, Jane; you're doing a rotten job of making yourself feel better.

Without meaning to, she couldn't help but think of what Peter had spoken of when he didn't know she was listening. Was her father really once a friend of his? Was he some kind of honorary Lost Boy, or at least, he used to be?

She tried to imagine her father as a kid, running with Peter and the gang after a giraffe or something, unafraid of crocodiles or time or Pan. Before he broke.

Jane always knew her father was a good man. Maybe he wasn't all good, and maybe he didn't often let it show at all, but she was sure of it. She'd seen it. And those moments, those precious moments when he proved he was good, she clung to them with all her heart. She'd never forgive herself for forgetting them.

Someone touched her shoulder, making her flinch. But one look and she realized it was her father. He was looking at her with concern on his brow. Jane nodded, knowing this was just a warning, not a sentiment.

Hook gave the signal.

The cannon fired with a deafening boom.

Jane clutched her pendant.

The crystal hit the sea with a splash, somewhere past the center of Cannibal Cove. Ripples grew and diminished. Then the water began to churn.

"Mister Smee," Hook called, eyes shining as the whirlpool became stronger, "pipe up the crew!"

"Aye aye, Captain!" Mister Smee saluted, sending up the call, "ALL HANDS ON DECK! PREPARE TO WEIGH ANCHOR!"

Jane took a deep breath, as ready as she'd ever be to set sail into a swirling massive portal.

● ● ●

CHAPTER TWENTY
THE PLAN COMMENCES

When the first ship raised anchor and disappeared into the whirlpool, Alice was the only one who could see it. When Jack and Red asked what was going on, she tried to explain the scene as best she could.

"It *disappeared*?" Jack questioned from the other side of the mast.

"I think it went through a portal," she responded, heart sinking.

The crew bustled about in a rush, barely paying them any attention as they prepared to lower the sails and raise the anchor. Thankfully, it seemed they were on one of the last ships to leave. That gave them more time to either escape or be rescued... Either that or it just gave them more time to dread every second of swirling water pulling them to its center.

Well that wasn't a very positive thought.

"How's it going with the ropes, Rubes?" Jack whispered.

"*I'm trying*," Red hissed back.

"Try harder," Alice pressed as another ship went sailing toward the portal.

Red struggled with the bindings. Alice had long given up on the prospect with her own ropes; they were too thick, and her inexperience with the unfamiliar knots only rubbed the skin off her wrists. There were easier ways to free herself.

There was a shout that made her jump.

"Uh, guys, something's going on," Jack spoke up from his view of the docks.

"What's happening?" Alice questioned, hopelessly straining to see for herself.

"Do super tall pirates usually break in half after tripping over wheelbarrows?"

"*What?*"

That's when chaos struck.

*****

Originally, the plan was to wait until someone was aboard the *Jolly Roger* to reveal themselves and attack. Unfortunately, this wasn't exactly the best plan Kai had ever thought of.

There were a few things going for them, though. With the overcrowding, no one noticed the extra pirates in shady hats and trench coats slinking into Blind Man's Bluff. And in the chaos of resupplying ships, the increase of large covered carts was easily overlooked. Never mind they were strategically placed and guarded by these unfamiliar men.

The problem was Kai.

The way he walked with purpose, the way his eyes glowered, the way the scar on his jaw shone like a jagged battle wound; he looked every bit a captain. He made to cover the length of the port, searching for the names of each ship he passed. Because of his age and unfamiliar face, he didn't have to wear such a large hat as the others did.

Leaving the dock of another ship that failed to be the *Jolly Roger*, Kai felt a chill shoot down his spine. He locked eyes with the man who stared at him. His stomach tightened as he realized his face wasn't as unrecognizable as he'd thought.

It was the pirate he'd met in the jungle. Kai still had the knife he'd stolen from him at his belt.

"NOW!" Kai thundered as loud as he could.

Wild cries rang through the air in response. One glance around and he saw the rescue mission thrown into action. Trench coats opened to reveal multiple Lost Boys on each other's shoulders. Tarps were ripped off the carts, letting loose a stream of Panther warriors decorated in elaborate war paint.

There was only one moment of shock and panic before the pirates pulled out their weapons.

Whirling around, Kai rushed for the harbor to board a ship. Before he got far, the brute who knew his face pounded after him. With a shout, he rammed right into Kai, knocking both to the floor. Kai twisted himself around as soon as they landed, threw himself at his attacker and sent them rolling and struggling across the dock. Drawing his dagger, he managed to get enough control of the situation to hold the blade against the man's throat. But he grabbed his wrists and shoved him away, sending them sprawling once again.

With a last heave, the pirate forced himself on top. Kai tried to stab him in the stomach, but the knife was knocked out of his fingers and scattered out of his reach. Large hands gripped his throat tight, cutting off his air. Struggling, Kai pushed against the pirate's face, bit it was no use. This opponent was bigger than him, stronger than him. Changing tactic as stars speckled his vision, he desperately tried to pry the beefy hands from his throat.

Stars darkened to swimming blots.

The man sneered. He might've said something, but everything was ringing static.

Air suddenly flooded his lungs just as the pirate was yanked away screaming. Choking, gasping, Kai shook away the fuzz in his eardrums. The ticking wouldn't go away.

Raising his head, his heart plummeted at the sight, scrambling backwards.

In a panicked mania, the pirate was being dragged off by a gigantic crocodile that had him by the foot. The beast ignored the wild flailing of his victim as they slipped into the sea and out of sight.

Crimson clouded the water just off the dock. Kai felt horrifyingly sick. He'd have to keep his wits about him and ears open for the Crocodile if he didn't want to be the next meal.

And where did that whirlpool come from?

For the Twins, fighting on each other's shoulders was a given. It gave them a thrill, and the confusion on the pirates' faces: priceless. Swinging cutlasses with apparent carelessness, one faced one way while the other faced the opposite. Then they'd swap.

No blood spilt, double stacked, watch the feet, careful 'round the head; what a game!

Now, where was the challenge?

"You know," one Twin called down, "I bet I can knock out more pirates than you. Duck!"

He leapt up just as his brother ducked, a blade sweeping between them just in time.

"No way," the other exclaimed as he kicked a pirate in the shin. "I've knocked out way more already!"

"No you haven't!"

"Yes I have!"

"I can knock out much more!"

"Is that a challenge?"

"Bring it!"

"*Oi!*" Slightly snapped from across the street. "You two, focus! Besides, I'll be knocking out more than the both of you combined."

The Twins looked up and down at each other, grinning mischievously. The call was simultaneous: "You're on!"

Slightly pulled his crooked grin, whacking a pirate over the head with his bow. "ONE!"

*****

"Hurry!"

"Come on!"

"Just give me a *minute!*" Red snapped.

They were all far too antsy about the escalating battle, and Jack wasn't exactly great for commentary. Not only that, but according to Jack, it didn't seem like this rescue party even knew where they were. And Alice worried the line of ships raising anchor was getting shorter.

Ropes tangled in her fingers, Red felt she was about at the point where just the right pull would slip the whole knot off. "Almost..."

"You can do it," Alice persisted, clearly anxious.

"... Got it!" She exclaimed as her hands yanked free.

Jack gave a whoop.

Quickly, she turned to untie the others, wrestling with the bonds. Attention so absorbed in the complicated knots, she completely forgot the crew.

Jack shouted the warning, "Red, look out!"

Before she could react, strong hands grabbed her wrists and yanked her away from the mast.

"Oh, no, you don't," the pirate growled, clamping a heavy cuff to her wrist despite her struggles. Then he bustled away with a sneer.

Red yanked at the iron chain attacked to the deck, but it was no use. It was bolted fast, and now she couldn't reach the others. With a groan, she tried to search the surrounding area for anything to pick the lock with. She didn't want to break her thumb if she could avoid it.

*****

Kai would've been decapitated if Tootles hadn't fired his slingshot. The rock hit his attacker smack in the forehead, forcing her to stumble back in shock. Whipping around just in time, Kai caught her before she fell on him, grabbing her neck just right until she slipped out of consciousness. He managed to push her onto a bench out of harm's way.

Tootles had already vanished.

"KAI!"

Nibs was at the end of the block, staring at the port with growing worry. Kai jogged over quickly.

"What?"

"It's... the *Jolly Roger*," he stammered anxiously, pointing. "I think it's about to raise anchor."

Kai scanned where Nibs was pointing, finally finding the bloody ship. Of course; it was the auburn one at the other end of the harbor. The *Jolly Roger* had the sails lowered, the crew hurrying about the deck frantically.

He'd never make it on foot.

"You've got to fly me over to the ship," Kai determined.

Nibs huffed, "I couldn't carry you *walking*! You can't expect that to change with me *flying*."

He pretended he didn't just hear that.

"Look, Curly's right over there." Nibs nodded over to the giant Lost Boy. "He can take you."

Before Kai could argue, the kid turned on his heal and dashed back into the chaos. He scratched his scar agitatedly. Sprinting for Curly, he closely avoided a tribesman and his tomahawk.

The boy swung his club around like a maniac, no one able to get closer than an arm's length away. Kai dropped to a crouch just as the heavy weapon sailed over his head.

"Curly!"

He turned toward him, dropping the club. "What?"

"I need you to take me to the *Jolly Roger*," Kai explained, standing straight.

A pirate charged. Kai almost sprang to action, but Curly whipped around, hoisted the man off his feet, and used his momentum to toss him over his shoulder. Kai jerked out of the way. With a crash, the pirate landed smack on his back, groaning in blank shock.

Kai blinked.

Curly looked back at him as if nothing happened. "Let's go."

Tiger Lily did not like restraining herself. This was ridiculous! The fewer the pirates, the better they would all be. But the Lost Boys insisted that only Pan had the authority to permit a slaughter. So, begrudgingly, she gave her warriors the order not to kill unless absolutely necessary. It was only a precaution. She did not want to test the law of Pan lest the Island decide to enforce it, or punish her people for disobeying it when in allegiance with the Lost Boys.

Even so, despite having to hold back the entirety of her ferocity, Tiger Lily was a force to be reckoned with. Movements remained quick, sharp, and cautious. The Lost Boys stayed clear of her as if she would mistake them for the enemy. This with the combination of war paint around her eyes and the feathers braided into her teased hair made her fearsome, a terror.

The pirates were getting away, boarding their ships, sailing into the sea. They needed to take them, as much as they could. But even with the Panther Tribe and the Lost Boys, the pirates outnumbered them, and unlike them, the pirates didn't have regulations against slaughter. Thinking quickly, Tiger Lily gave a shrill whistle loud enough to reach Neverpeak Mountain if the right ears listened.

She heard the screams and smiled.

The panther bounded through the chaos to her side, scaring off her attackers with a yowl. Bagheera waited expectantly for instruction.

With a few barking commands in her own language, Tiger Lily managed to spread the word to her other warriors about her plan. They obediently joined her, a mass barreling through Blind Man's Bluff toward the closest ship. Bagheera protected them, using his weight and claws to his advantage.

They stormed the ship, taking the pirates by surprise. The crew hastened to scramble away from prepping the ship to defending it.

• • •

"Lock them in the brig!" Tiger Lily shouted in the chaos.

Something caught her eye, drawing her attention. She frowned. Was that Curly flying off over the harbor? But who was that clinging to his arms?

Deciding not to bother herself with the Lost Boys' childish affairs, she returned to overthrowing the ship.

CHAPTER TWENTY-ONE

THE PIRATE SHIP

It was as if the battle down in Blind Man's Bluff jarred something in Jane, making her push aside all her conflictions and leaping into action. It was a pirate's life for her. It always had been. Now, it was almost as if she'd never left. But the torn bits, the part of her that still recoiled at the Bird's words, the part of her that still broke at the look in Peter's eyes, she kept them hidden away. Growing up with pirates, she learned it was never a good idea to show any sign of weakness. They'd pick you apart like vultures.

"I need men up on the mainmast," Jane barked, demanding order. "Ready the sails! Prepare weigh anchor!"

"All that time with those devils; you're sure you haven't lost your touch, brat?" sneered the peg legged pirate, Skylights.

Blood boiling, she shot him a deadly glare. "Give your insults ground to stand on or sound like a fool. Questioning my loyalty might be the *stupidest* thing you've ever said. Do that again and I'll string you up by your toes and feed you piece by piece to the Crocodile."

"Need I remind you who you're talking to?" Skylights growled, straightening to his full height. It was moments like this where she really wished she was taller.

Jane planted her feet, undaunted. "Need I remind *you* who you're talking to?" she threatened. "Know your place, Mister Skylights. Or need I remind you what happens to pirates who cross me? If I need to take your other leg, too, it won't nearly be such a clean cut."

Narrowing his eyes, Skylights shifted on his wooden leg. He didn't nag her anymore; probably didn't want another stain on his pride. Knowing he wouldn't dare question her authority again, Jane went back to barking orders as if nothing happened. Skylights merged in with the crew to fulfill them.

Rain had started falling, slow and steady. Jane looked up at the sky as if it were a final blessing from Neverland, a farewell of sorts, instead of the Island's possible reflection of Pan's mood. But the water was her domain. Hers. Water was the life or death of a ship, and the ship was the life or death of a pirate. So the rain didn't discourage her. It enthralled her.

"Prepare weigh anchor!" she exclaimed again with renewed passion.

As soon as she turned around, she found herself facing a visitor. She scowled.

"Who in Neverland are you?"

Kai landed on the deck of the *Jolly Roger* with a thud, ungracefully catching himself with his hand to avoid landing on his face. The drop jostled his ankle so much he had to wait a moment to recover. The crew was too busy to really notice him. Looking up, he saw that Curly got his foot caught in the rigging and was trying to wriggle himself free.

A rush of movement grabbed his attention, and with a jolt, he had just enough time to raise his sword as the sharp blade crashed down on him. He caught a glace of his attacker: dark eyes framed by black hair.

Sylvia?

Deflecting the blow, Kai rolled out of the way and jumped to his feet. Who was this girl? It wasn't Sylvia... There was something around her neck, a damaged wooden pendant. He knew it. He'd seen it before, in a memory that wasn't his.

"That's her," Curly called down, jerking out of the rigging. "That's Jane."

Jane.

Kai frowned. "You're Hook's daughter?"

She looked at him strangely, sword raised and ready. Then she attacked, metal ringing in the air as Kai switched to defense.

Barreling his way below deck, Curly called back, "I'll search the ship for the others."

"You go do that," Kai managed, ducking under the sweep of Jane's cutlass.

She lunged, forcing him to jump back and deflect the blow. He hardly had time to breathe.

Don't hurt her; don't get killed.

She wasn't making that easy.

"Why isn't your crew cutting in?" Kai questioned, knocking aside her sword.

"Bad form," she said simply. "I can take care of myself."

Her blade swung over his head just as he ducked.

Jumping back up, Kai tried to explain, "Look, I don't want to hurt you."

"How sweet. Can't say the same about you."

Sword swinging, they crashed so hard it sent vibrations up Kai's arms. Jane remained unfazed, continuing relentless attack. Her fighting method was too sporadic and unfamiliar. If he wanted to survive, he'd have to switch the offense. She never allowed him opportunity to do anything but block.

"They're not on the ship," Curly boomed as he emerged from below deck.

Jane smiled at that.

Curly eyed the situation. "Need help?"

"No," Kai gasped when he almost got gutted. "No, I'm good."

Jane raised an eyebrow, lunged. Kai went to block, but she swept her sword back at the last second, wrapped her bland around his, and yanked it free from his hand, sending it clattering across the deck. She held her sword to his throat, black hair plastered to her neck with rain water.

Kai wanted so desperately to reason with her. He'd made a promise not to hurt her, but that didn't stop her from wanting to kill him. "You don't have to do this."

She stared at him, conflicted; he could tell by the way her brow twitched. But he knew her decision before she did. Her arm was too steady, and he was still a stranger to her. In one movement, Kai dropped to the ground and rolled out of range from her thrust. Curly swooped towards him, grabbed his arms, and flew them off the ship. Jane gave a frustrated cry as the two tumbled back into Blind Man's Bluff.

"Dude," Curly laughed, "you just got creamed."

Kai picked up the closest sword he could find. "I know."

There was a roar of victory at the other end of the harbor as Tiger Lily's warriors took a ship. Kai nervously looked at the remaining ships. Which one had his friends held captive?

Bells rattled through the rain. Three fairies zipped up to him, dodging raindrops and jingling frantically. There were two he didn't know, but Tinker Bell right up and perched on his shoulder. One of the fairies suddenly plummeted when a drop hit her square in the back. Kai's reflexes caught her just in time.

Tink instantly started ringing in his ear urgently.

Kai turned to Curly. "Do you know what she's saying?"

He shrugged. "I can try. Say it again, Tink."

The pixie began again, the bells in her voice much slower.

Curly furrowed his brow. "She either says that she can't see very far, or she knows where they are."

Tink groaned, giving him some lip.

He grimaced. "*That* I understood. I'm going to assume you're just frustrated and didn't mean it."

"You know where they are?" Kai questioned anxiously.

Tink and her friends nodded vigorously. The third fairy pointed back towards another ship, the name bright despite the rain: *George Nicholas*.

Curly gave the fairies some trinkets in his pockets to keep them dry.

"Tell the others to meet us at the ship," Kai instructed before they flew up and away. "We're going to need back up."

*****

Of course, her hands were too tightly fastened for her to reach the knife hidden in the back of her pants. Even so, if

Red could keep mercilessly trying to pick the lock on her cuffs, Alice could at least do her best to get it.

The rain was falling, a nuisance to Jack who apparently stood under a post that poured water directly on his head. He made a point to complain about it regularly in the midst of his commentary of the fight below. But Alice's heart leapt as soon as the ropes around her wrists slipped. Her fingers touched the knife's cold hilt.

Backing up against the mast, the sharp prick from the blade pressed against her spine. She suppressed her gasp, frozen. Shock subsiding, she strained again to grab it, lips pressed tight, metal piercing her skin, blood tickling her back.

Sorry Remus, she thought, hoping it didn't hurt so bad on his end.

Finally, she grasped the hilt and carefully pulled it from the scarf around her waist. Clutching tightly, she slowly moved her fingers to arrange the knife in the right place. She sawed at the ropes, holding her breath every time a pirate came by. Numb fingers stung from the pricks she gave herself.

Just as the knife broke through, someone landed on the deck in front of her.

"Kai!" Red exclaimed, dropping the heavy chain.

He grinned, then whirled into a duel with the pirate beside him.

"What am I, chopped liver?" the Lost Boy proclaimed.

"Curly, isn't it?" Jack called over.

"Yeah, yeah," he grumbled, whacking a charging pirate aside with his club.

Their rescuers busy fending off attacking pirates, Alice took the opportunity to yank herself free from the mast. Jack stared at her when she came around to free him. She just shrugged, pulling off the last of the ropes.

"You get the key for Red," Alice insisted, giving him the knife.

"What are you going to do?"

She grabbed the nearest weapon she could find: a wooden plank. "I'm taking the ship."

Kai broke out of the duel with a kick to the man's groin. "Where's Wendy?"

"They're both in the brig," Red spoke up, nodding to the entrance to the lower deck.

A pirate stormed for the escaped prisoners. Swinging the plank, Alice smashed it into him, sending him back a few steps. Before he could attack again, Red threw her chain around his neck and pulled taunt.

"Get on it, then!" she pressed, holding the man hostage until he fell unconscious.

Alice took the man's cutlass and set to work.

Wendy's head snapped up, neck sore.

"Did you hear that?" she asked.

Peter groaned from the ach when he looked up. The anchor was weighing him down. "Hear what?"

There was a crash, louder this time, somewhere above deck. It was definitely not her imagination. The ship jerked under her feet, throwing her smack to the floor. Before she could pull herself back to her knees, the ship jolted again. Peter shouted as that one sent him over just enough to be pinned to the ground with the anchor on his back.

● ● ●

Breathing heavily, Wendy hoisted herself back up.

"Are we moving?" he questioned, squashed.

She shook her head, eyes to the ceiling. "I think we've stopped."

Creaking eerily, the hatch opened. Wendy tried to brace herself for another encounter with Jane or Hook or more pirates ready to beat them to pieces. Something came crashing down, heavy, tumbling down the stairs. The pirate landed right in front of her, flat on her face. Peter and Wendy stared at her, but she didn't move.

The following figure was very much active. "Wendy?"

She blinked, making sure she was seeing things properly. "Kai?"

He grinned, some kind of heavy mallet in hand.

"I'm here, too!" someone shouted down from the top of the stairs.

Peter twisted his head around, chin propped. "Is that Curly?"

"No, it's Cubby—of course it's Curly!"

"You feeling unappreciated?"

"I don't need your sarcasm, Pan."

"I appreciate you, Curly," Wendy called up with a smile.

"Thanks, Wendy."

Kai came to her first. "Hold still." Hefting the mallet over his head, he brought it down right on the chain, metal screaming. He only had to do it four times before one link broke and he could pull the chain out from her detached cuffs.

Wendy shook out her aching arms, the cuffs now like aggravating bracelets. "How'd you do that?"

"Weak link," Kai shrugged. "I was a blacksmith, remember?"

She laughed, threw her arms around him and squeezed tight.

Curly stomped down, dangling the ring of keys in his hand with a raised eyebrow. Without a word, he unlocked Peter from his chains and heaved off the anchor. Rubbing his wrists, Peter scrambled to his feet. Wendy met him just as he clasped his arms around her, holding each other.

"So you're the Pan?" Kai commented.

Pulling away, Peter nodded. "Peter. I'm guessing you're Kai."

He grunted affirmatively.

Wendy let Curly unlock the cuffs from her wrists. "And the others?"

"We got them; they're taking the ship."

"By themselves?" Peter questioned.

Kai just shrugged. "We'll see when we get up there."

● ● ●

CHAPTER TWENTY-TWO
BLAZING CANNONS

Tink and Sparrow flew as fast as they could while carrying Hazel between them. She held the mushroom, the only useful thing Curly had given them.

The problem with getting the word out fast was that the only people who could understand them were nowhere to be found. Tink looked around quickly and led them towards the first Lost Boy she found. Unfortunately, that happened to be Slightly.

"Just start shouting," she advised the others. "Get his attention."

So they tried jangling as loud as they could—in fact it was the loudest she'd ever heard Sparrow speak. But of course, Slightly wasn't paying a lick of attention. He was too focused on launching those ridiculous cloth-covered arrows at unfortunate pirates. They did nothing but stun until he could get to them himself.

Tink rolled her eyes in annoyance. He was counting again! *Another festering challenge...*

"SEVENTEEN!" he cried happily as another pirate collapsed.

Deciding to take care of this nuisance herself, Tink helped Sparrow find a dry spot to set Hazel before whizzing off to get the stubborn Lost Boy's attention. She yanked his orange hair and pinched his neck, trying to get him to notice her.

"Slightly!" Tink chimed in a passion. "Slightly, you stupid oaf; answer me!"

She finally whacked him in the face with her mushroom umbrella, repeatedly. That got his attention.

"Ouch, Tink," Slightly whined. "You know, sometimes, you can be really mean. What's gotten into you?"

"Curly and what's-his-name need you!" Tink cried out. "They need back up!"

He looked at her blankly.

Tink smacked her forehead. *He doesn't understand a single thing I'm saying.*

Of all the Lost Boys...

She started again, speaking slower and using vigorous and extravagant hand motions. *"You* need to *go* over *there."* Tink pointed from Slightly to the ship, then whipped her arms around. *"Bring* more *Lost Boys."*

He scratched his head. "You want me to throw everyone in the water? Or, you want me to jump in the water and give everyone a hug?"

"No, you good for nothing, mud brained, *doofus!"* Tink shouted, kicking her legs in frustration.

"No need to get all feisty," Slightly grimaced. "Unless you're complimenting me instead of what I think you're saying."

Tink glared at him, flying up to point clearly to the ship. *"There!* You need to go *there!"*

"We need to go there?"

Tink groaned and nodded. "Yes!"

"Well, why didn't you say so?" He grinned stupidly, the arrogant toad. Then he bellowed out to the others, "Oi! Move to the *George Nicholas*! I've got a feeling Pan needs a new crew."

• • •

229

Slightly charged for the ship, Lost Boys from all over following behind him. The whole lot took up a wild whoop of delight as they barreled for the boat. Tink gave an exasperated sigh as she fluttered over to join Hazel and Sparrow in watching the battle play out.

Boy, did she love those idiots.

*****

Rushing into the Captain's Quarters, Jane stated, "They've escaped. They've taken the *George Nicholas*."

An enraged roar rattled her eardrums, making her want to curl into a ball like a child. Hook chucked a bottle across the room. Glass shattered upon impact with the wall. She cringed at the outburst. She waited silently, shutting the door behind her, a hand on the handle just in case.

"Blast it all!" Hook bellowed, raking his iron hook across his desk. Wood shavings curled up from its path. "That darn Pan! I should've killed him when I had the chance!"

Jane bit her lip, unsure whether she was disappointed or relieved he hadn't. "The *Jolly Roger* is ready to set sail. The men are raising anchor as we speak."

"We can't go now; don't you see?" he cried. "We'll be arriving empty handed!"

"No, we won't," Jane insisted. "We have a whole fleet of ships and pirates already there. We'll add a tremendous amount to the army awaiting us, and the Shadow—"

"What use are ships where we're going?"

"What use are *we* if we stay and get ourselves *killed*?" Jane argued. She knew that above all else, she did not want to face Peter again. And when she thought of the boys... Curly would barely even look at her. Best get as far away as possible.

Hook looked her in the eye. Bloodshot. Again. That explained the bottle.

"If we go," she continued, knowing how to deal with this, "we still have a fighting chance to live and a definite chance at revenge."

Realization came over his face, clearing the fury. "Yes, of course. Why hadn't I seen it before? If we leave, I'm not sacrificing my revenge, only postponing it. It's brilliant!"

Jane smiled to hide the hurt that the thing that drove him to save himself wasn't the threat on her life, but the assurance of his vengeance. Fortunately, she knew how to hide it, and he was too drunk to notice anyway.

"Are we to continue through the portal, then?"

His eyes sparkled. "With our cannons blazing."

*****

"Prepare to set sail!" Peter crowed. "Twins, Slightly, Nibs; lower the sails."

"Yes, Captain," the Twins saluted, scampering up the mast like raccoons.

"Curly and Kai, man the cannons," he ordered. "Take a group with you."

"Aye aye," Curly bellowed.

"WEIGH ANCHOR!"

Jack helped turn the great wheel with the others, pushing and heaving until the anchor was raised from the depths.

"Red, Alice; you two keep a lookout up at the crow's nest," Peter called after asking Wendy again what their names were.

She tugged at his sleeve, realizing the mistake. "Uh, Peter, it might not be such a good idea sending Alice up there."

"Why not?"

"She has a bit of a problem with, uh, *heights*."

"Oh."

Looking down from the quarter deck, Peter informed, "Change of plans. Red, keep a lookout up at the crow's nest; Alice, up at the bow."

"Yes, sir," Alice sighed in relief, practically skipping to do his bidding.

"The rest of you should know what to do." He planted his feet and readied himself. "Batten down the hatches! It's going to be a bumpy ride."

The sails dropped, billowing out as they caught the wind. Slightly flew up and raised the colors: that being a pair of bright purple britches waving in the air. The *George Nicholas* swept out after the *Jolly Roger*, swirling current pulling the both of them in. The tribesmen in the docked ships yowled triumphantly as they passed.

Peter gripped the wheel so tightly his knuckles turned white. A dangerous fire in his eyes, he set his jaw as they pursued the *Jolly Roger*.

The wind picked up, growing vigorous, whistling in Wendy's ears. She looked up as soon as the sky broke loose to let the rain shower upon them.

As if we weren't already wet.

• • •

Lightning cracked, making her jump, the following thunder just a formality. Waves washed up against the ship's sides. The water churned faster, pulling them in. There was no going back now.

"Why does it have to be raining?" Jack exclaimed, slipping across the deck below.

"Haven't seen a storm like this in ages," one Twin called out.

"Pan must be really riled up," the other added.

A blast louder than thunder split the air. The cannonball hit the foremast at full speed, wood flying, causing the whole thing to topple over to starboard. Another cannonball shot past Tootles and splashed into the water.

"THEY'RE FIRING AT US!" Red shouted down from the crow's nest.

"I think we've got that, Rubes," Jack called up at her.

Wendy thought she saw Red stick her tongue at him, but she couldn't be sure from this far away.

"LOAD THE CANNONS!" Peter thundered. "PREPARE TO FIRE!"

Wendy leapt from the quarter deck, running to the entrance of the gun deck and trying not to slip. She relayed the order to those below, Curly and Kai instantly barking orders. They were all trying to stay on their feet in the chaos. Grabbing a bit of rigging, Wendy waited, watching those below.

Nibs ran past with a cannonball in his hands, zipping out of sight. Then back came the cannonball with Nibs chasing after it.

"Alright, hurry up," Kai commanded. "Get these cannons loaded up and prepare to fire!"

• • •

"What he said," Curly agreed.

Wendy couldn't help but smile when Nibs pounced on his prize, hustling over to the nearest cannon and dropping the ball in the barrel. Kai positioned himself beside a cannon, ready to light the wick. Even from her distance, Wendy could see the *Jolly Roger* come into view through the porthole.

"FIRE!" Peter shouted from above.

"FIRE!" Wendy echoed down.

"LIGHT 'EM UP!" Curly bellowed.

All wicks lit at once. Wendy braced herself, covering their ears. The blast echoed through the whole ship as cannonballs took to the sky.

"HIT THE DECK!" Red cried from her perch.

Wendy threw herself to the ground, rolling over and hitting the grate as cannonballs flew at them. One nicked the bulwark, sending up a shower of splinters before it rolled across the main deck. Two flew overhead and hit the water with a splash. But another hit the mainmast, causing it to teeter dangerously. Wendy saw Red hold tight as she swayed due to the damaged mast.

"Red!" she cried, scrambling to her feet.

"I'm fine," Red hollered down. "We hit them!"

Wendy whipped around. Sure enough, the mizzenmast of the *Jolly Roger* was hanging over port. Jagged holed gaped on its side. Her eyes widened, realizing how close the two ships were getting, and how close the center of the whirlpool was. Was the light down there dimmer?

She rushed to the quarter deck to join Peter, but Kai was suddenly there, frantic.

"Pan!" he shouted.

"I'm a little busy at the moment!" Peter cried as he struggled with the wheel against the current.

"That portal is going to close any minute," Kai warned, rain running off his nose. "If we don't hurry, we're in for a lot of water."

"What are you suggesting?"

"We follow them into the portal. It's our only chance."

Pan nodded in understanding.

Wendy sighed, leaning over the railing to scream, "BRACE YOURSELVES!"

Everyone hurried about at her warning, hanging on tightly to the ropes and the bulwark.

We've had way too much experience with this sort of thing.

Wendy clung to the railing, Kai throwing his arms on either side to lock her down. With a shout, Peter whipped the wheel around, sending the *George Nicholas* barreling towards the *Jolly Roger*. The bow hit them in the stern, lurching both ships forward into the portal. Holding tight, Wendy looked up to see the whole thing. Light swallowed the lot of them, forcing her to squint. Even so, all she could see was light and shapes.

The crack of splintering wood filled her ears, and a scream split the air. Wendy's stomach clenched at the sound. Something swept to the side, giving another deafening crash. A shot sounded somewhere in the chaos, barely audible. She almost wasn't sure she'd even heard any shot.

A gasp of fresh air hit her lungs for a spit second. Instantly, the air pressurized, compacted, and became impossible to breathe. Her ears popped. Suddenly, the ship thrust backwards. Roaring water crashed around them. The ship burst from the portal and out of the sea, water washing out over the deck. The force jarred through her shins. With a start, Wendy realized she was completely soaked.

Peter pulled himself to his feet, blinking away water. "What happened?"

Wendy looked around. The *Jolly Roger* was nowhere in sight.

"We're still in Neverland."

CHAPTER TWENTY-THREE
"DON'T SAY GOODBYE"

"A little help here!" Red shouted, hanging on for dear life.

Wendy hastened over to the bulwark to take in the scene. The mainmast had toppled completely over, leaving Red dangling from the crow's nest like a fish on a hook. Wet wood was not helping for her behalf. Unfortunately, she couldn't drop into the water and swim to shore; the ship had emerged clear on the other side of Cannibal Cove. Red looked down and let out a shriek, tucking up her legs. Wendy followed her gaze, stomach tightening. An open maw waited directly below her, sharp teeth shining in the sunlight. The ticking sounded mockingly counting down the seconds until she'd fall.

"Get me down from here!" Red screamed.

"Rubes," Jack called, appearing right beside Wendy, "just hang on!"

"You think I'm not already hanging on?!" she barked.

Wendy hated how helpless she was. If Jane hadn't stolen her happy thoughts… But the Twins were already hovering over Red's head, circling.

"Hang on," one of them laughed. "That's a good one!"

"Just *hang on*," the other mimicked. "We're coming for you, little Red."

Red froze stalk still. Did her face get paler?

"If you *ever* call me that again," she hissed coolly, "I will personally remove your all of your toes."

"That's too bad," a Twin quipped. "We quite like our toes."

"She's a little touchy, isn't she?" the other acknowledged.

"A bit snappish for someone dangling over the mouth of the ole Crocodile."

"Just get me out of here!" Red snapped.

"There she goes again."

"Boys," Wendy called over, "enough torturing her. Bring her over."

"Awe, but we were having so much fun!" one whined with a pout.

"Alright, fine," the other Twin caved. "Just *hang* in there, Red."

"We've got you."

"Yeah, you'd better," Red growled as they grabbed hold of her arms and carried her back to the ship.

When the Twins set her down on the main deck, Wendy sighed in relief. Red practically kissed the deck in delight.

"You alright, Rubes?" Jack asked, rushing to her side.

"I'm fine."

Looking back over the bulwark, Wendy watched the ticking Crocodile sink back into the water and disappear. That beast always seemed to show up. It was like a constant reminder, a dark omen, always there, always waiting.

Wendy turned away from the water just as Slightly swooped down beside the Twins, arms crossed and smiling arrogantly. "Alright, boys; how much did you get?"

The Twins grinned, stating at once, "Thirty-seven."

The number wiped the smile clean off his face. *"Thirty-seven?* I only got nineteen!"

"You snooze, you lose," one of them mocked with a shrug.

"No, I didn't lose!" Slightly insisted. "How much did you get each?"

The other Twin shook his finger at him. "No, you bet that you could knock out more pirates than the *both* of us."

"Therefore, we won," the other added.

"It goes without saying."

Slightly's mouth hung open. "I don't believe this."

"Well, you'd better believe it."

"You should know better than to make a bet with us."

"We will accept full slave duty to us 'til a giraffe enters Hangman's Tree…"

"Or your dessert until Neverland snows…"

"Or public humility until a star falls."

"Your pick!" They both grinned.

Slightly groaned. "I'll take humility, then. Seems shorter."

The Twins stalked off mischievously. "We begin in the morning."

Wendy laughed to herself. Kai joined them, walking with a limp, helping Red to her feet. Then it hit her.

"Have any of you seen Alice?" she questioned.

She only received shaking heads and confused looks as a response.

"Wasn't she sent to the bow?" Jack spoke up.

With growing concern, Wendy turned and ran across the ship, the other three following behind. At the bow, she couldn't see Alice anywhere. What if she went overboard? What if she fell into the other side of the portal?

Then she found them, Tootles kneeling beside Alice who sat against a pile of crates. Alice's eyes were squeezed shut, clutching her right shoulder, blood blossoming beneath her palm. Tootles examined the other side of her shoulder. Crimson stained her blouse.

"Alice!" Wendy rushed to her friend's side. "What happened?"

Tootles shrugged, keeping pressure to the wound. Alice opened her eyes, face contorted in pain. The others joined quickly, Jack dropping down beside Tootles.

"Remus is going to be very confused," Alice almost laughed. "I've never been shot before."

Red knelt beside Wendy, face grim. "I have."

"Who shot you?" Wendy questioned, trying to see the wound. *Please don't be fatal.*

"Someone over on the *Jolly Roger* fired his pistol when we were in the portal," she answered. "I happened to be in the way."

"Did the bullet hit her lungs?" Wendy asked Tootles.

He shook his head, beckoning Jack closer, grabbed his hand, and placed it over Alice's exit wound. When Jack took his place in applying pressure, Tootles scampered off. Kai followed.

Red took a look at the wound. "It's a flesh wound; you'll be fine."

"Peachy."

Jack looked up at Wendy, whispering, "She's gone crazy."

"I can hear you," Alice spoke.

● ● ●

"I know."

When Tootles and Kai returned, they were dragging a damaged sail behind them, tearing it to strips for bandages. Chewing the inside of her cheek, Wendy reached out to pry Alice's hand away from her bullet wound. Alice's hand was shaking. Removing the scarf around Alice's waist, Wendy used it to press against the entry wound. Tootles came over with the makeshift bandages. He bandaged the padding in place around her shoulder, under the armpit, across the chest. Wendy helped by instructing what to do. Red moved out of the way, standing beside Kai, watching.

Jack was stuck where he was.

"How are you feeling?" he questioned, awkwardly moving his arm from Tootles to duck under.

"For a girl who's just been shot, I'd say I'm doing fairly well." Alice answered, smiling way too much for a girl in pain. "Unless you count the pain, the loss of blood, and the massive headache as *bad* things."

"I thought I was the funny one."

"You can keep your title. I'm delirious."

"No, *crazy*, remember?"

"Wendy teases, Red's sassy, Kai's sarcastic."

"Really? Sarcastic?"

"Don't start," Kai muttered, coming over to loop the sling he made over Alice's neck.

Tootles tied off the bandage, helping her arm into the sling. She thanked him, earning a smile. Wendy caught him in a hug before he could scamper off again.

With no mainmast or foremast, and the time it took for the entire flock of their peculiar crew to push them both off—and even then it wasn't until the pixies arrived to shower the fallen masts with pixie dust did they manage it—sailing back to Blind Man's Bluff took a little longer than it should've.

The pixies reported the happenings in Blind Man's Bluff. Three ships were taken by Tiger Lily's warriors, with only four reported casualties on the pirate's end. Two Lost Boys and a handful of tribesmen were injured, but Alice seemed to have the worst of it. And all the pirates were locked in the hold of each ship. They were to be dealt with later, once the *George Nicholas* arrived.

After helping shove off the floating foremast, Jack parked himself beside his best buddy who seemed very interested in nothing in particular over the bulwark. "Hey."

Kai grunted a greeting, obviously distracted.

He folded his arms over the railing, watching the waves. They weren't needed for the crew; Pan and the others were taking care of that. Besides, Jack wasn't sure he'd be much help. This was the first time he'd ever been on a boat this big.

"So, what did I miss?" Kai asked at last. "After the dragon, I mean."

Jack almost laughed. "Uh, well, I think Wendy and Rubes got captured by Tiger Lily's gang, ended up convincing her to take him back to Pan. They made a deal that landed us in this mess."

Kai nodded, like it didn't surprise him. "What about Alice? Did she get into trouble?"

"Not that I can make of it," he admitted. "She ended up with the pixies; the only good spot on this bloody island."

"Lucky."

"I think she's making up for it."

He grimly agreed. A pair of purple britches floated past the ship. Jack decided not to question it.

"What about you?" Kai questioned.

"Rescued Nibs from some pirates and a cougar, then convinced him to take me to Hangman's Tree," Jack explained with a shrug. "The girls were already there when I arrived."

He raised an eyebrow and huffed a laugh.

Jack ignored that. "And you?"

"Got faulty directions from a pirate, ran into those blasted sirens at the lagoon. Then a Neverbird rescued me and took me to Skull Rock where I encountered ghosts."

"Ghosts?"

"Ghosts."

Jack heaved out a breath. "That's rough."

"You have no idea," he mumbled. Before he could allow any time to dwell on that, he stood straighter. "Since when do you call Red that?"

"What? Oh." Jack rubbed the back of his neck. "Nibs suggested it. Kind of. Seems more fitting than an acronym, don't you think?"

Kai just grunted in response.

"DROP ANCHOR!" Pan's voice boomed.

Jack turned around, finding Blind Man's Bluff just off port. The ship jerked to a stop, docking in place. Lost Boys leaped over the side to tie the cables to the harbor. Tribesmen waited for them, helping secure the ropes that were too heavy for the kids.

Peter grinned down at them all from the rigging. "All ashore that's going ashore."

● ● ●

It took Wendy three tries to explain everything, the things they'd learned in Wonderland, the Master Hook had flown to. Tink spoke up about her news of some force gathering dangerous followers to build an army. Wendy's stomach clenched at the thought.

How much more are there?

But then Tiger Lily spoke about the army, how if there was an army, there must be a battle. Wendy wondered how much she knew about the matter, if she knew anything at all. Even so, it shocked her when Tiger Lily said her tribe would fight.

"Does this mean the alliance is still intact?" Peter questioned, raising an eyebrow.

She gave a sharp nod. "If a battle is coming, you need allies. So long as the Hook is following this terrible force, my people will fight it." Pausing briefly, she narrowed her eyes when Nibs kicked another pebble away. "Even if we must side with children."

Her warriors stood erect in agreeance behind her.

The light shone off the pocket watch's silver casing in Alice's hand, catching Wendy's eye. She swallowed the lump in her throat. Grabbing Peter's hand, she pulled him aside to talk to him somewhat privately.

"What is it?" he asked.

She licked her lips, finding it so hard to get the words out. "I need you to do something for me. I can't do it myself."

"Anything."

"Tell my parents I'm safe," she pleaded. "And that I'll see them again after this is all said and done."

Peter frowned. "Wait, but—"

● ● ●

"I'm going with them." Wendy nodded over to the others, ready to take the watch wherever it brought them. "I have to. This... force wants us, the five of us. I can't leave them. And if Tink is right, then this is bigger than we thought, and we need to stop it."

He looked like he wanted to protest, try to convince her to stay. But he didn't. Wendy sighed, thankful for it. She was afraid she couldn't leave if he asked her to stay.

"I'll tell them," Peter promised. "They probably won't believe me, but I'll tell them."

With a grateful smile, she kissed him quickly, squeezing his hand. "Thank you."

He kept hold of her hand as she turned to rejoin the others to say farewell. She hardly got a word out before the Lost Boys surged forward like a mob, everyone wanting to hug her at once. Holding them tight each in turn, she assured them she'd be back soon. It was only temporary. But Wendy wasn't sure that promise was more for their comfort or her own.

The pixies zipped up, too, Sparrow and Hazel jangling their goodbyes. Tink couldn't get anything out, her glow was so scarlet. She finally just hugged her thumb, pinched her nose, and flew over to sit on Peter's head.

As soon as she gave the last Lost Boy a hug, Wendy emerged from the crowd and ran right into Peter's arms. She couldn't hold back the tears anymore. He held her close, burying his face in her curls.

"Don't say it," he whispered.

"Don't say what?"

"Don't say goodbye."

He once told her what goodbye meant, what it always meant to him. It meant going away; it meant forgetting. Perhaps Hook feared time above all, but Pan feared of forgetting, or more importantly, of being forgotten.

"Goodbye doesn't have to mean forgetting, Peter," she said softly. "I will always believe in you. And that's more powerful than memory."

When she pulled away, Wendy gave him an encouraging smile. Pulling a dimpled grin, he let her go to the others who waited for her around the pocket watch.

She looked at her family one last time.

Red pushed the button.

CHAPTER TWENTY-FOUR
THE WINDOW

There was a corner house in Bloomsbury, the kind of house people liked to stare at because of its charm, the kind of house people liked to imagine the life inside. Lights always shone somewhere in the windows as if no one ever went to sleep. And the nursery window was always open, calling for visitors. No robber would dare enter, though. Open windows only meant there was a guard watching.

Indeed, the Saint Bernard was the first to enter the nursery every night, sniffing each bed with careful precision. His inspection complete, Porthos sat promptly in the center of the room as soon as the door burst open again. A little boy ran in, the stuffed bear in his hand barely able to keep up. He laughed, greeting Porthos with a pat on the head and a kiss below the ear. Wagging his tail, Porthos followed the little boy around the room.

"Peter," his father called just as he stepped into the nursery carrying a chunky baby girl. "Come on, Pete, time for bed."

Pete squealed in protest, rolling over the floor. Porthos took the opportunity to lick his face, earning abundant laughter.

"Michael, give me little Maggie," the lady of the house insisted as she emerged from the doorway.

Michael passed the baby over to his mother's outstretched arms, diving after his son. Catching up the boy, Michael blew on his soft belly. Pete erupted into giggles, encouraging the zerberts. The lady chuckled to herself.

Bouncing the baby on her hip, she let Maggie pull on her grey braid.

Buzzing him around like a fighter jet, Michael tossed his son into his bed. Pete struggled against the blankets. As soon as his teddy was tucked under his arm, he calmed down.

"Tell me a story, daddy," he pleaded, wriggling his thumb into his mouth.

"Not tonight, Pete."

"Please!"

Michael sighed, turning around to where the lady lay the baby down in her crib. "Mother?"

"I think the boy needs at least a song," she insisted with a smile.

So Michael sang a gentle lullaby to his children. His mother smiled at the words, lyrics telling about fairies born of laughter and laughing stars. When Pete fell asleep, Michael was still singing. He kissed his little forehead, crossing the room to press a kiss on Maggie's cheek.

"Asleep at last," he breathed.

"Oh Michael." His mother shook her head, giving him a kiss on the cheek. "Children should never go to bed. They just wake up a little older."

Michael smiled, wishing her goodnight before sneaking out of the nursery and switching off the light.

The lady took up the tune in a soft hum, going to each nightlight that guarded three beds. Turning them on, she kissed the sleeping children in turn. Except the dog. He only got a scratch behind the ears.

Pulling her chair to the middle of the room, she sat down to face the open window. The breeze rushed in, causing her to pull her robes snug. She could almost hear her husband snoring downstairs by the telephone.

The stars winked outside over the clock tower. They sang the lady to sleep, even though she tried to wait up as always... just in case.

Having done their part, the stars gave a shout to the boy waiting on the roof. The fairy went in first, a light illuminating the room. She buzzed over the children's sleeping faces. Porthos looked up to sniff her as she flew by, but he sneezed from the pixie dust the fairy left in her wake.

And then the boy flew in through the open window. Stepping down from the windowsill, he walked across the nursery floor to the woman asleep in the chair. He almost smiled at the nostalgia.

"I know you," he said gently, dimples deepening.

The fairy zipped up to sit on his shoulder, her light illuminating his face.

"What do you think, Tink? Should we wake her?"

Tink jingled a response, a voice behind the bells.

He nodded. "I suppose you're right. She'll probably think this is all only a dream in the morning, though. But a promise is a promise."

When Tink spoke again, the lady awoke at the sound of her voice. Blinking dreamily, she looked up at the boy. It was as if she'd been expecting him.

"Have you brought my daughter back?" the lady asked him.

Solemnly, he shook his head.

"Is she safe?"

"Yes."

"Will I see her again?"

"She promises it. When all is said and done."

The lady covered her mouth like she couldn't decide to smile or cry. Instead, she looked up at the boy again. "I love her."

"I love her, too."

"You once told me we couldn't both have her."

He smiled at his feet, a sad smile. "I've changed since then, I think."

She cocked her head. "Yes. You've grown up."

He grimaced at that, an instinct he'd probably never shake. Even so, she could see it. He was barely a boy anymore.

Looking over the beds along the walls, the lady made one last request. "Don't take my grandchildren. My heart can't break anymore."

He nodded silently, turning towards the window again. Tink swirled around the lady a few times. Her eyes widened in wonder. When the fairy joined the boy again, it was on the windowsill. Despite herself, the lady stood in shock.

But the boy paused, brown eyes looking back over his shoulder. "I never meant to hurt you."

Then he stepped off the railing and vanished. She rushed to the window, leaned over the side, afraid to find a body on the pavement. But there was nothing. Lifting her face toward the sky, she saw a star shoot across the night.

"Look after my Wendy," Mrs. Darling wished, eyes closed, "Peter Pan."

CHAPTER TWENTY-FIVE
CURSED CLOCK

Jane hung her head, hands folded in front of her. She didn't like the way those heterochromia eyes looked at her and her father. It made her want to curl up in a ball.

"What have you brought me?" her father's master questioned.

I suppose this is my master, too, now.

But Hook didn't tremble under that glare. Instead, he just raised the lantern by the claw, the dark mass swimming inside.

The woman in the corner gave a sharp laugh. "That's it? I knew you could never trust a pirate to fulfill an order."

Hook sneered at her, but it was Jane who snapped, "Obviously you can't pull through either, *Your Majesty.* Having difficulty betraying your own siblings?"

"Watch your tongue, little wretch." The Queen's eyes shot daggers.

"At least we managed to catch them," Jane pestered. "You couldn't even do that."

"They slipped right through your fingers... or claw."

"This," Hook rattled the lantern, "will hinder them in the long run."

"Oh goodie, we're chasing shadows now."

"ENOUGH!" the Master's voice echoed all around them, jostling their bones.

Jane clamped her mouth shut. She noticed the glare the Queen of Hearts gave them, though, despite her quiet.

Exasperated, the Master sighed, "I take it they're no longer in Neverland?"

• • •

"I wouldn't expect they'd stay," Hook reported.

There was a smile, a pleasure Jane didn't expect.

"Then everything's going according to plan."

*****

Colors muddled together in a great rainbow explosion. Ticking rang in Wendy's ears, a sound more powerful and chiming than the Crocodile's tocks. The rush didn't cause nausea, surprisingly, but she felt a collide of emotions she couldn't determine. Golden needles spun like a whirlpool around the pearly face, around and around and around...

The hands froze on a jewel star. Colors vanished. Silence screamed.

They dropped, or seemed to, with a jolt that shook her shins. Wendy landed flat on her back, the breath knocked out of her. Trees stretched up overhead, thick and old. Branches vainly tried to block the sky from view. When she recovered, she rolled over to get up. Broken glass touched her hand, scratching a finger. With a scowl, Wendy pressed her thumb against the small wound to stop the bleeding.

She looked around.

Red stood across from her, eyes wide, breathing rapid, face white as a ghost. She looked like she was going to fall over, but she was frozen. Was she going into shock?

"Are you alright?" Kai asked in concern, hastening to his feet.

Alice tucked the pocket watch under her shirt, approaching the stone faced girl cautiously.

"That cursed clock brought me back," Red breathed, hands starting to tremble. "*Here*, of all places, it took us *here*."

Wendy tried to take in the scene, piecing it together: the trees, the glass, the buzz in the air.

Rubbing his bruised head, Jack sat up, blinking back spots. "Where are we?"

Strangely, Red didn't snap about his inattention. But her response was nearly inaudible, "*La forêt enchantée.*"

Wendy frowned. She didn't know Red spoke French.

But she spoke again, louder now in translation, "The Enchanted Forest."

ACKNOWLEDGMENTS

As always, I want to thank my amazing family for their constant love and encouragement. Even their pestering for this book and the next feeds my thrill of storytelling. I'm not sure writing a series would be nearly so enjoyable without them. My family is a persistent reminder that anywhere can be a home so long as I'm with them.

Thank you to my friends all around the world! You have all helped shape me into the person and writer I am today. Your friendship has shown me that it's not the place, but it's the people who can make anywhere I go something like a home.

My thanks go to the wonderful authors J. M. Barrie, Hans Christian Andersen, and Lewis Carrol, as well as the unknown storytellers of "Little Red Riding Hood" and "Jack and the Beanstalk" for blessing this world with their marvelous stories. I am so blessed to have the privilege to use their stories in my own way. I hope I've honored their memory.

It was also a joy to acknowledge a flavor of Rudyard Kipling's "The Jungle Book" by including his characters' namesakes, as well as a nod to the fairytale "Cinderella", and include the brilliance of Robert Louis Stevenson's "Treasure Island" which I cannot wait to expand. Though not all were prominent in the book, their magic was fun to include.

Thank you to Aleshyn_Andrei for one of the stunning images that make up this cover, as well as Derek Murphy with his helpful tips in DIY book covers. Thanks to my proofreaders who help me see the glitches I couldn't.

● ● ●

And thank you to all of the people who have shown excitement about this series! You, dear reader, are such a blessing to me.

All of my thanks goes to my Lord God, who has and is and always will be with me through everything. Above all else, I do what I do for Him. May He receive all glory.

Get ready for the next adventure...

The Realms Series

Book Three

The Enchanted Forest

Emory R. Frie

...Coming Soon

Emory R. Frie is the award winning author of her debut novel, *Heart of a Lion*, and her new fairytale rewrite, *Wonderland*, the first installment in The Realms Series. Emory is attending Berry College to further pursue her writing craft. Raised in Oregon, Emory now lives in South Carolina with her family, Scottie dog, and retired barn cat.

Made in the USA
Monee, IL
30 September 2020

43621372R00152